ABOUT SA

CW00403673

"Sally Jenkins knows how ... *mundane, and makes it intriguing. She hooks the reader, and reels him in ... her capacity for twisting each tale's ending is nothing short of phenomenal."* - Readers' Favorite Book Review Website.

Sally's stories have been successful in a range of competitions and magazines. She has twice won the Friends' of Morley Literature Festival Short Story Competition, was the 2014 Disney Winnie the Pooh Laureate of the Midlands and in 2016 was shortlisted in the Just Write Creative Writing Competition.

Sally has written two psychological thrillers. *Bedsit Three* won the Ian Govan Award and was shortlisted for the Silverwood-Kobo-Berforts Open Day Competition. Of *The Promise* one reviewer wrote, *"There is something about the way that Sally Jenkins writes that draws me in and keeps me wanting to read more."*

Sally lives in north Birmingham with her husband. The wilderness of Sutton Park is close by, a wonderful place for wandering, plotting and creating characters. By day Sally works in IT but after hours she lets her imagination run riot. And when she's not hammering at the keyboard she gets her exercise bell ringing and attending Bodycombat classes.

Follow Sally Jenkins on Twitter: @sallyjenkinsuk
Find out more about Sally and follow her blog at
http://www.sally-jenkins.com

One Day for Me
Old Friends
House Guests

SALLY JENKINS

One Day for Me

Old Friends

House Guests

Guest Story: Salvation Copyright © 2017 Iain Pattison

All other stories: Copyright © 2017 Sally Jenkins

ISBN 13: 9781521418246

ALL RIGHTS RESERVED

All content herein remains the copyright of Sally Jenkins, 2017.

The right of the author to be identified as the author of this work has been asserted by her in accordance with the relevant copyright legislation in her country of residence and generally under section 6bis of the Berne Convention for the Protection of Literary and Artistic Works.

This book may not, by way of trade or otherwise, be lent, re-sold, hired out, reproduced or otherwise circulated without prior consent of the publisher or author.

This work is a work of fiction. Name, places and incidents are either products of the author's imaginations or are used fictitiously. Any resemblance to any event, incident, location or person (living or dead) is entirely coincidental.

For further information and details about volume sales, please see the author's website at www.sally-jenkins.com.

One Day for Me

SALLY JENKINS

CONTENTS

ONE DAY FOR ME

Winner of the 2011 Friends of Morley Literature Festival Short Story Competition
Shortlisted Writing Magazine Crime Story Competition 2010
Commended Lichfield and District Writers' Short Story Competition

Her face didn't look like that of a murderer. It was the face of a plain, 57-year-old woman with a slightly too large nose and prominent crows' feet. Moisturiser, make-up or anti-wrinkle cream hadn't touched it for decades. Staring at her brightly-lit reflection, Lillian blinked like a tortoise emerging into the first sunshine of spring.

The hair salon wasn't the cosy housewives' refuge she remembered. It had morphed into an impersonal space of black leather chairs, harsh music and grey marble sinks. But it did exude the luxury that Lillian craved.

"You haven't had a professional haircut for thirty years?" Leo sounded interested rather than shocked.

In the past Stanley had hacked at her shoulder length hair with the kitchen scissors but Lillian wasn't going to explain Stanley to Leo.

The hairstylist gathered her greying locks in his hands and drew them away from her face. "A short bob would suit you."

As she reclined her head backwards into the basin, strong fingers massaged her scalp. Her head tingled with increased blood flow and then she was draped in the thickest towel she'd ever experienced.

Leo worked quickly and soon she was an island in a sea of grey waves.

"Some blonde highlights would knock years off you. What do you think?"

For three decades no-one had noticed Lillian. Today she was going to put that right. Her budget was limited to the cash in Stanley's wallet but Leo didn't need to know that.

"Sorry. I haven't the time."

Her cheeks reddened even though it wasn't a complete lie. If she had the highlights she would miss her manicurist's appointment.

Leo's fingers brushed her forehead as he styled her fringe. She shivered – no-one had been so physically close to her for years.

Stanley hadn't come near her since his affairs started so there'd never been any children. A week before their first anniversary he'd come home smelling of another woman and six months later he'd suggested separate bedrooms. His mistake had been to insist that she still brought him morning tea to bed. She remembered the shock on his face as she had delivered more than just a hot drink only a few hours earlier.

Leo brushed and curled and the heat from the hairdryer tickled her neck. Then he shielded her eyes to spray her new style into place before holding a mirror behind her so that she could admire his handiwork.

"Thank you."

Lillian smiled as she handed over Stanley's £20 notes and felt giddy with euphoria as she left the salon. Today was her first day out alone since her husband caught her having tea in a café with a neighbour, twenty-nine years earlier.

"What a blatant waste of my money when we only live around the corner."

Since then she'd been under lock and key whilst Stanley was at work or otherwise engaged with his lady friends. He'd dressed her from charity shops and accompanied her around the supermarket. She'd lived on a diet of daytime TV and the odd newspaper that he'd brought home.

Was this queasy, light-headed feeling something that all prisoners experienced on their release? Or was it anxiety about what she had to do later?

Tracey, the manicurist, didn't look old enough to have left school. She despaired over the state of Lillian's hands and recommended rubber gloves and an expensive make of hand-cream or, preferably, the purchase of a dishwasher.

Then she started trimming and filing, accompanied by a stream of mundane chat.

"Have you been on holiday?"

"No."

"What are you doing for Christmas?"

"Nothing." Lillian had never done anything for Christmas except cook and wash up and it wouldn't change where she was going.

"Nice weather we're having."

This small talk was difficult. Stanley never attempted conversation. He muttered orders to her and shouted at the television.

Tracey stopped shaping and moisturising and presented Lillian with a brilliant array of nail polish colours. It was like an army trampling over her senses. Caught in this strange 'now or never' day, she seized her last chance to be a scarlet woman and chose the brightest red.

Three neat strokes and her thumb was the colour of blood.

Lillian's heart hammered and her hand trembled as it had when she'd wielded the knife that morning.

"Keep still or I'll smudge it."

Her unpainted hand clenched as she remembered that knife penetrating his chest, the scream and his eyes locking on hers. The more she'd stabbed, the easier it had become and the less he'd struggled. Then he didn't move and his eyes stared but didn't see her. It had all been so simple because he was still half asleep.

The blood would have ruined the mattress and probably the carpet as well but it didn't matter because neither of them would live there again.

"Other hand, please."

Who would clean up? That and disposing of the body hadn't featured in Lillian's planning of today. There was only one important thing that she still had to do. Pride wouldn't let her do it looking like a misfit created by her dead husband.

The two coats of colour plus a top clear layer took forever. Once outside, Lillian plunged her hands deep into her coat pockets. The red nails signalled to everyone that she had her husband's blood on her hands.

The cash in Stanley's wallet wouldn't stretch to the posh boutique on the High Street but Marks and Spencer was luxury enough.

The clothes were displayed in colour coordinated racks and it was easy to pick a skirt, jacket and blouse that matched. She dismissed the greys, greens and browns as too much like Stanley's sensible charity shop stuff. Instead she marched towards the changing room with an armful of purples and pinks.

"Hello, Stanley's wife isn't it?"

Lillian felt like a balloon pricked with a pin.

"I've seen you in the supermarket with him. It's so good of you to support our charity shop the way that you do. What a shame those terrible migraines stop you getting out but we enjoy helping Stanley to choose your outfits."

"Pleased to meet you." Lillian could only manage a weak smile for the woman who had selected her second-hand wardrobe.

"We've got some lovely winter coats in the shop at the moment. I was going to point them out to Stanley next time he comes in. But why don't you have a look later?"

"I haven't the time." Lillian edged towards the fitting room.

"Have you done something to your hair? It looks nice."

Lillian wrenched the curtain across the front of the cubicle and sank onto the stool. She touched her burning cheeks. How many other lies had Stanley told to excuse her absence from everyday life? She'd never suffered from migraines but could feel a headache coming on now.

Her red nails flashed before her as she slipped the soft blouse from its hanger. Dark plum varnish might have been a better choice.

It felt almost sensuous to be wearing brand new clothes that both fitted and suited her. They covered up the hurt of the last three decades. She reluctantly peeled them off and went to the cash desk.

Now Stanley's wallet held just enough for a final coffee and cake.

She'd already decided on the most expensive café in town but first she must look the part. Lillian slipped into the shopping centre toilets as second-hand Rose and emerged as a confident butterfly. She'd slicked on some of the lipstick sample that Tracey, the manicurist had given her and the perfume counter girl had sprayed her with something classy.

Last time Lillian had been in a café it had been a choice between coffee and tea, now there was a whole page of cappuccinos, lattes and espressos. The waitress tapped her notepad with a pencil whilst Lillian struggled to decipher the menu.

"A chocolate éclair and a large cappuccino, please."

They drank cappuccino a lot on the television so it seemed a safe choice.

The éclair's cool, creamy centre and sticky sweet topping swept Lillian back to her courting days when Stanley had wooed her in cafés and restaurants and taken her on trips to the seaside. But now she understood how he operated. As soon as he'd hooked one girl he became bored and moved on to hunt the next. None of his affairs lasted very long. That was why he'd never got rid of her. He needed a cook, cleaner and occasional punch-bag. Lillian always knew when he'd been dumped by one of his other women because he took it out on her.

The cappuccino was disappointing; the froth was cold and the coffee too strong. Lillian spent a few minutes scraping the bubbly remnants of the drink with a teaspoon. Police station coffee was probably going to be much worse than this. Then she emptied the contents of Stanley's wallet on the table and left.

"I stabbed my husband to death this morning."

The desk sergeant raised his eyebrows.

"Before he drank his morning tea, it must still be there, at the side of the bed." This small detail suddenly seemed important to Lillian. "He always had two digestives as well."

Lillian was ushered into a small room. There was a table and tape-recorder, as she'd expected and a uniformed constable stood by the door. She perched on the edge of a hard chair and waited, a smile on her lips as she remembered her day of freedom.

She'd sung in the shower for the first time. Then she'd taken Stanley's wallet and walked into town in the autumn sunshine for her hair appointment. Her heart still glowed from the close contact she'd had with Leo and Tracey, even the desk sergeant had been pleasant, considering what she'd told him. The meeting with that woman from the charity shop had been unfortunate but she'd coped.

Lillian straightened her fitted skirt, swept a stray hair from her eyes and placed her manicured hands on the table. She radiated pride. Today had been perfect. Stanley alive had meant solitary confinement at home. Stanley dead meant prison and a chance to mix and make friends.

The future looked bright.

REPLACING THE EMPIRE

Second place Snapshots of History Autumn/Winter 2012 Competition
Included in The Green Silk Journal Winter 2012

"How can a woman be a whole empire to a man?" Wallis fingered the neck of her silk blouse. "I can't go ahead with it."

She sat down on the window seat and stared out at the sweeping drive.

"But you're dressed and ready. We're all ready ..." Emerald's voice was agitated. "Edward will be waiting for you. Surely this is just last minute jitters."

"Emerald darling, this is the third time we've done this. You know I don't suffer nerves when I'm sure what I'm doing is right."

"But how can this be wrong when Edward has publicly declared and demonstrated such a deep love for you?"

"I feel suffocated by his expectations. He has given up his whole life for me – what can I possibly give him in return? I will have to spend the rest of my life trying to please him."

Emerald began to wring her hands. "He made me swear, as your matron of honour, to look after you this morning and deliver you safely to him. He called you his Empress."

A flush penetrated Wallis' wedding make-up.

"That's his pet name for me." She dabbed her eyes with a handkerchief. "But now it sounds kind of hollow. It's just another expectation that I can never fulfil."

It was Emerald's turn to stare desolately out of the window over the lawns of the French country house towards the sweeping driveway.

"The cars are arriving. We must go downstairs."

"No, I need more time. Edward received a letter last night from the King and it upset him greatly. Although he's no longer entitled to it, George is going to allow him to keep his 'Royal Highness' title."

"That's good news isn't it?"

"George's generosity never comes without a condition. And this time it is that I am not to share the title and in the unlikely event that we produce children, they won't be entitled to it either."

"That's hardly a great surprise is it?"

"No, but Edward has taken it as a personal insult to his future wife and heirs. You see how much pain he continuously bears on my behalf? I can't carry on being a millstone around his neck."

"Pull yourself together, Wallis!" There was a new determination in Emerald's voice as she picked up her gloves and checked her hat in the mirror. "There's no going back. The abdication is signed and sealed and George is King. If you back out now then it will all have been for nothing."

A sharp knock at the door made both women jump.

"They're coming for me!" declared Wallis like a woman about to be executed. "Tell them I need a few more minutes."

The door opened before Emerald had a chance to reach it.

"I need to do the pre-ceremony photographs, Mrs Simpson."

"Yes, of course. Do come in, Mr Beaton." It was as though a veil of composure had passed instantaneously over Wallis' previously fraught and tense face.

As Cecil Beaton set up cameras and lights, Emerald arranged the simple silken rose headdress in her friend's dark hair and pinned the antique brooch at the high neck of Wallis' fitted blouse.

"I expect most of the weddings you attend are grander than this, Mr Beaton," remarked Wallis as she posed on a red velvet chair, her hands in her lap. "Proper society weddings have shoals of pastel bridesmaids and kilted pageboys and acres of veil for the innocent bride to hide behind."

"I find the simple weddings are often the most enjoyable," said the photographer quietly as he expertly packed away. "Now, I'll leave you two ladies to your preparations. I have to catch His Royal Highness as he arrives downstairs for the ceremony."

"If Edward hasn't yet arrived that gives us about fifteen minutes," said Emerald. "Let me clip that headdress on a little more securely. It's breezy outside."

"But Edward is never late. He must have decided I'm not worth it!"

Wallis slumped on the chaise-longue, her shoulders heaving and soft sobs falling into her handkerchief. Eight months ago she had wanted to marry the King of England more than she'd ever wanted anything in her entire life. But the roller-coaster ride of his abdication had cooled her enthusiasm. She had felt powerless as he had ignored her pleas to remain as monarch and since then she had felt attached to him with a ball and chain. But now he was rejecting her! The tears came unchecked and she felt like a knife was tearing at her self-worth. Rejection was a new experience.

The telephone on the side table gave a loud ring and Wallis sat up. Emerald grabbed the receiver from its cradle.

"Thank you. I'll let her know." She said into the handset and then turned to Wallis. "He's arrived! That was his valet and Edward wants you to know that today is the start of the happiest days of his life."

Wallis stared at her friend, the drying tears leaving her make-up streaked. Her eyes registered relief but a frown began to crease her forehead and thin painted red lips.

"You see – his expectations of this marriage are huge! How will he survive without the family and country to which he was born? How will I survive without the society and parties that drew me to him? He loves me too much but without his royal status I can't love him enough. I fell in love with the King of England not a disgraced minor royal."

"Things will get easier when recent events have

been forgotten. King George will forgive and forget – after all he's reached an office that he always thought out of reach."

"Queen Elizabeth will never forgive us."

"Time is a great healer. Now, let me repair your make-up."

"No need. I'm not getting married. I shall write Edward a letter and then disappear back to America."

Wallis shrugged off Emerald's attentions and sat down at the writing bureau. She picked up a silver fountain pen and a sheet of heavy headed notepaper. She wrote with a fluent and confident flourish, aware of Emerald hovering but not quite daring to read the emerging letter over her shoulder. Now that she had made the decision Wallis felt in control of her life again and she felt her shoulders relax and the lump in her throat disappeared.

"What shall I tell them all?" Emerald's voice had become small and nervous.

"You tell them nothing," said Wallis firmly. "Just hand this letter to Edward and he will deal with it. Cancelling a wedding shouldn't be difficult for someone who was supposed to rule the British Empire."

She signed the letter and carefully blotted the notepaper without rereading her words. Then she folded it to fit the thick cream envelope.

"HRH Duke of Windsor," she muttered to herself as she addressed it. "My feelings shouldn't come as a surprise to him. I explained I couldn't live up to his expectations before he renounced the throne."

When Emerald had left to deliver the letter Wallis removed her headdress and shook her hair free. Edward was handsome, generous and fun –

everything she looked for in a society playmate. If pressed on the point she would even admit to loving him, which hadn't been true of her previous two husbands. But her shoulders weren't strong enough to cope with the pressure of replacing everything that he had given up for her.

The bang on the door made Wallis jump to her feet. Edward strode in and slammed the door behind him. His eyes blazed and his mouth was set in a tight line.

"I have no expectations of you, Wallis Simpson." The harsh but quiet tone of his voice did not invite conversation. "None at all. I decide my fate just as you are free to choose yours. I agree that a woman cannot be a whole empire to a man. However; few men have an empire bigger than their own back garden and they are content with that. Why should I be any different?"

"Because you had a taste of that empire." Wallis touched his hand to try and diffuse the anger within him.

"All marriages are a journey into the unknown, as you should know." Wallis thought she caught a twinkle in his eye as he said these last words. "I know your track record and I'm willing to take that gamble. Without the burdens of state, my shoulders are light and I have no expectations of you other than the occasional kiss."

Wallis felt his arms go around her slim waist and she raised her mouth hungrily to his.

"But you do know that you can't abdicate and eat it, don't you," she whispered as they pulled apart.

He laughed, pinched her bottom and left the room before she could slap him.

"Shall I redo your make-up?" asked Emerald, coming back in through the still open door.

"Yes, please." Wallis smiled at the thought of her true English gentleman.

THE LONELINESS OF THE SHORT DISTANCE RUNNER

Winner Freelance Market News 'Fireworks' Competition 2012

Shona is raising her arms above her head and waving at the athletics stadium crowd. The commentator is telling us this is the local girl who's made the big time. She grew up less than a mile away and now she's competing here, on an international stage.

"Look at Mummy," I say to Daniel.

He yelps with excitement and tries to stand up on my lap. Shona is on the start line around the other side of the track and so we have to watch her on the big screen. I examine her face in close up and try to spot any signs of this morning's row.

"Sparkles?" Daniel asks me, pointing at the screen.

"The fireworks come at the end of each race," I explain.

He's remembering the last time we watched Shona run at a Diamond League meeting and a mini pyrotechnic display erupted above the big screen after each event. That competition was Shona's big comeback after taking two years out when she became pregnant with Daniel. She didn't down tools completely, she never does, but allowances had to be made for the unborn baby and then for her body to return to 'normal'. All that time it was like living with a caged lion. Shona hated not being able to push her body to its limit and she missed the adrenaline of competition.

"Set."

The athletes raise their hips and extend their arms. The stadium is silent.

"Go! Go! Go!" shouts Daniel and jumps on my thighs, impatient to watch his mum fly round the track and unleash a fountain of coloured sparks into the evening sky.

I hold tight to his waist so that he can't fall and try to ignore the pain in my thighs every time he bounces in his new leather shoes.

***

"Focus, Shona, focus!" I urge myself.

My muscles are tense and ready to fire me from the blocks. My ears are straining for the gun but instead I hear the faint wail of a baby in the crowd.

"Shut up!" I mutter. "Let me concentrate. This isn't the time for babies."

There's a pang in my heart as I realise that's the phrase I used this morning to Robert. "This isn't the time for babies."

We were rehashing the argument that's been reverberating around the house for almost a week.

Robert didn't understand that another baby meant two more years out of top flight competition. It would put my place in the next Olympics at risk. Talented youngsters are streaming through the athletics clubs' ranks and into the national squad all the time. I can't afford to let my guard down at all. More children have to wait until my active athletics career is over. Then I can coach or commentate and have another child. Lots of women have babies in their late thirties nowadays.

Robert won't accept this plan.

"Everything revolves around you!" He'd exploded at me this morning. "What about me? What about Daniel? We have to fit around your training regime. We have to put up with you jetting off here, there and everywhere. You won't even marry me because the wedding preparations will play havoc with your schedule."

That baby wails again somewhere. I touch my stomach and my determination about the future wavers. A baby or a gold medal – it's a stark and lonely choice to make.

Focus, Shona, focus. The gun is about to go.

Then it does.

***

I see Shona react a split second after the rest of the field. I hold my breath.

"Bang, bang, bang," Daniel mimics the sound of the gun and waves his arm about, two fingers pointed, like he's a cowboy in the Wild West.

Shona's fighting to overcome her hesitancy out of the blocks. Is that bad start my fault for stirring things up again this morning? I shouldn't have done it, not on a race day.

"Mummy!" shouts Daniel.

I pull him down into a sitting position and squeeze him closely to me. I wish I could do the same to my unborn child, the tiny fluttering of life that is accelerating round the track in Shona's womb. Time is running out for that little scrap of humanity. She wants to flush it away like we did with Daniel's goldfish when it died.

"It's not the right time," she said, showing me the plastic stick with its blue line.

Her voice shook and there were tears in her eyes. I thought I could change her mind but after the initial shock she hardened her heart. Shona's got her career mapped out and there's no room for mishaps – even if they did happen in the name of love.

Daniel wasn't planned either but back then she felt young enough to be able to make a comeback and still have time to achieve her goals.

"It's just a clump of cells," she said to me this morning, like she was trying to convince herself as well as me. "It's no different to having a tooth out."

How can she believe that?

Now the athletes have reached our side of the track. Seven skinny women in Lycra pants and skimpy tops are vying to be fastest. Disciplined hours in the gym have moulded their muscles and flattened their stomachs. Raw ambition defines their lifestyle, diet and private life. The rest of us take a poor second place.

She knows we're sitting here but she won't look.

***

Forget the bad start. Go forward. Accelerate around the second bend. Keep the speed up don't relax. Robert and Daniel are here somewhere, don't look for them. There's a twinge in my stomach. Someone's on my shoulder. Concentrate. Focus on the movement of my arms as I head towards the 300 metre mark.

Now someone's on my other shoulder. Ignore that twinge in my stomach. The crowd are shouting. Their words are unintelligible. Need to save something for a sprint finish but can't let those two on my shoulders past. We're so close we could touch each other but each of us is alone too – fighting for individual glory.

Ignore the twinge in my stomach.

Tomorrow it'll be over. I've made the appointment. Won't tell Robert until it's done. No point starting another fight. Once it's gone he'll be OK with it. There's plenty of time in the future for babies.

Final 100 metres is coming up. Kick hard and pull away. Everyone's moving quicker. I need to move the quickest. Ignore the twinge in my stomach. Legs are on automatic. Strides are long. The noise is growing. We're all in a line as we cross the Finish. My legs crumple. Bright colours dance above the big screen. There's popping in my ears.

***

"Shona!" I scream louder than ever before as the first three runners breast the line.

People turn and look but I don't care. Shona should have won easily but it's turned into a photo finish.

"Sparkles!" laughs Daniel, waving at the rainbow of lights shooting into the air above the big screen.

The fireworks explode regardless of who wins. My son gives me a big grin and claps his hands.

Then I see that Shona is down. She's lying on the floor – too far away for me to see what's wrong. The baby, it has to be the baby. There's a stretcher coming out. I need to be with her. I pick Daniel up and push past the other spectators. They swear. I don't care.

We're allowed in the ambulance with her.

"Third," she mumbles. "All that work for all those years and I came a lousy third."

"Only by a fraction of a second. Next time you'll win." Automatically I try to make her feel better.

The paramedic monitors her blood pressure. My eyes linger on Shona's washboard stomach. From her prone position she puts an arm around Daniel's waist. She places her other hand gently on her tummy.

"I've killed it, haven't I?" Her voice is empty.

"Let's wait for the scan," says the ambulance man.

At the hospital a cheery lady takes Daniel off to find some toys and I watch the sonographer perform the ultrasound. Shona starts to cry as the inside of her womb appears in front of us. It's impossible to decipher the sci-fi image on the screen.

"I've got two heartbeats," says the sonographer eventually.

"So?" I ask, barely thinking straight.

"Twins – you're expecting twins."

"And they're not dead?" Shona sounds incredulous.

21

"They're most definitely alive but you'll have to take it easy for a while."

I hold my breath, terrified of what Shona might say now.

"That's fine." She's smiling. "I'm finished with giving up my best years to be beaten by a hair's breadth. It's lonely out there on the track and I can see now that some things are more important than chasing elusive gold medals."

Then she turns to me. "Robert, will you marry me?"

My internal score board turns gold and the sparkles rain down.

FOUND PROPERTY

Shortlisted Writers' News 'Going for Three' Competition 2012

It all started when she found the glove. It was just lying there, forgotten, on the bus seat.

"I found this." Charlotte offered it to the driver as she got off.

"Bully for you," he said, drumming his fingers on the steering wheel.

"Someone might go to your lost property office asking for it."

"Keep it, love. Anything worth claiming in our lost property gets nicked by the other drivers." He glanced over his right shoulder, to pull out into the stream of traffic.

Charlotte stuffed the glove into her pocket.

Next time she was on the bus she spotted a wet, half-folded umbrella under the seat opposite her. This time she didn't tell the driver. It was raining and the umbrella would stop her carefully straightened hair frizzing as she went to meet her mates at Valentino's.

"That umbrella's designer," said her mother when she spotted it drying in the kitchen the next morning.

"How can you afford stuff like that without a proper job?" asked her father. "Going to that ex-poly was worse than not studying at all."

Charlotte ignored him and took the umbrella upstairs. She typed 'used Louis Vuitton umbrella' into eBay. There were three on sale with prices ranging from £145 to £499. Hers was identical to the cheapest but in a slightly worse condition.

Within minutes she had photographed the 'found' umbrella both open and closed, uploaded the images and specified a starting bid of £75. Seven days later she posted the umbrella to its new owner for a final sale price of £120.

It seemed that if you played your cards right there was money to be made in found property. In fact it could become a business – as long as she didn't reveal too much to her parents about where she sourced her stock.

She had her own business cards printed to prove to her parents she was a proper entrepreneur. They were purposefully vague, stating 'Charlotte Simpson – Procurement Specialist' and included a pay-as-you-go mobile number and a webmail address.

"Shouldn't you have a 'Limited' or 'Director' on there, seeing as you run your own business?" her mother always found something to criticise. "It would make you look more professional and less 'dodgy'."

Charlotte shrugged, stung again by her mother's words.

"Audrey's son's got a lovely business card," her mother went on. "It's plastic, not cardboard. He's a professional musician. She gave me some – have one."

Charlotte reluctantly stuffed the plastic card in her jeans pocket. She hated her mother's constant unspoken comparisons between the successful offspring of her friend and her own daughter. Charlotte knew she always came off worst.

She rarely gave out any of her cards herself but her mother distributed them to all her friends, who dutifully added Charlotte to their email address books and now she got inundated with round robins about sick children, cute animals and unfunny jokes. It was a small price to pay to stop her mother nagging about 'finding a proper job'.

After graduating with a third class Media Studies degree from a university that her father always referred to as 'a polytechnic', a 'proper' job had been impossible to find. She'd tried stacking shelves in a supermarket and had a spell as a barmaid in the local pub but neither interested her, satisfied her parents or paid enough to make leaving home and their never-ending criticism even a dim possibility.

But since the glove, her prospects were getting better.

Charlotte began buying DayRover tickets, allowing her to ride buses across the city all day, and she devised a method for hunting down the lost property. She went upstairs first, remembering to look under the seats and pay special attention at the back - things had a habit of sliding down the bus. Then she sat at the rear downstairs and watched people, especially those with multiple bags and packages. When the driver was occupied with taking fares she would meander down the aisle and back scanning for forgotten items. She always carried a large empty shopping bag and became adept at swiftly slipping things into it.

Most days she found at least one chain-store carrier bag containing a brand new piece of clothing. If the receipt was in there and the customer had paid cash Charlotte returned to the shop and claimed a refund otherwise it went on eBay. Mobile phones were a common find too and Charlotte became pally with the man at the 'Unlock Your Mobile' market stall. He asked no questions about the number of phones that she brought him.

"What you do is your business," he said to her with a wink.

As if by way of explanation she gave him one of the newly printed business cards and he pointed people her way when they were after a cheap phone or iPod – she found lots of those too.

Charlotte was soon selling 'found' stuff regularly and could afford the rent on a small bedsit. It was grotty but it was away from the nosey prying of her parents.

"You must be doing something right in this procurement business," said her father grudgingly as he dropped her, her bags, laptop and half a dozen cardboard boxes of 'finds' at the bedsit. "I just hope it's not dodgy."

The first musical instrument Charlotte found was a clarinet, forgotten by a schoolgirl giggling with her friend as they got off the bus. Charlotte had a sudden vision of herself 10 years earlier desperately making excuses to her fuming father for the disappearance of her school recorder. She'd been forced to pay for it from her pocket money for months and months.

"Excuse me!" Charlotte followed the girl off the bus and handed her the clarinet. "You forgot this."

She found the next instrument on one of the bus routes near the university – students are notoriously careless with their belongings. It was on the floor, at the back of the top deck. The bus was empty and the next stop was the depot. If she left it, one of the drivers would nab it.

Back home, she placed the case on the Formica table and, as she opened it, a ray of sunshine burst into her dingy bedsit. The gleaming tuba smelled of polish and reflected Charlotte's yellowing lampshade, stained wallpaper and grimy window in its perfectly polished shine. Nestled in the black velvet interior of the case, it was the most obviously loved and cared for thing she had ever seen. It was too beautiful to touch.

Charlotte sat and marvelled at it.

The recorder incident flashed through her mind again but she didn't let her conscience prick for long – an instrument like this must be well-insured.

The top price for tubas on eBay was £3,250 and, given its immaculate, scratch-free condition this one had to be at the high end. Selling the tuba would provide the deposit plus a few months' rent on a nice studio flat. That would be one in the eye for her father.

She photographed the instrument, lifting it from the case with a towel so as not to leave fingerprints on the mirror-like sheen. eBay insertion finished, she made beans on toast and switched on the TV news.

"…appealing for return of his Cerveny tuba. As

well as being a very valuable musical instrument, it has great sentimental value to professional musician, Julian Wagstaff."

Charlotte stopped chewing. The TV presenter was standing outside a terraced house with a young man. There was something vaguely familiar about this thin youth, all dressed up in a bow tie and tailcoat, as if he'd been about to go on stage with his orchestra when the tuba had been snatched from his arms.

"My father bought it for me before he passed away last year," said the young man, looking as if he was about to cry. I'm offering a £500 reward."

The beans stuck in Charlotte's throat. Until now she'd had no conscience about selling her found property – after all, as that driver had told her, very little of it would've found its way back to its rightful owner. But seeing Wagstaff's grief was making her feel bad.

"If you do find it," the young man continued, "please don't remove the tuba from the case. It is a very delicate instrument."

Charlotte stared at the glistening metal and wondered if she'd damaged it.

The TV presenter was thanking Wagstaff now and wishing him luck. As the camera panned away Charlotte suddenly knew who he was – the son of the Lady President of her mother's golf club, Audrey. Charlotte had only met him once, at some sort of charity fundraiser that her mother had dragged her along to. Julian and some student friends had provided the entertainment.

He was the professional musician with the plastic business card.

This was Charlotte's chance to shine in her

parents' eyes. Returning the tuba would bathe her mother in reflected glory and even her father would have to admit that she'd 'done well'. Maybe she would donate the reward money to charity for extra effect…

Charlotte removed her internet advertisement and gently pushed the tuba back into its case. But it wouldn't fit. She used as much pressure as she dared but a lump beneath the velvet lining was hindering her efforts. Exasperated she thrust her hand down the gap between case and lining. Her fingers closed around a booklet. She drew it out. It was a passport – and the young man in the picture looked nothing like Wagstaff. She pushed her hand through the gap again and pulled out two more dark red British passports. These held pictures of oriental women and had issue dates in the future.

Charlotte smiled, contrary to her parents' opinion she wasn't the only off-spring from her parents' circle with a 'dodgy' business and Julian's dirty deeds might benefit her. She retrieved his plastic business card from her jeans and dialled.

"I have your tuba," she said.

There was a whoop of joy from Wagstaff.

"And your passports," Charlotte added. "I think we need to talk."

DEAL OR NO DEAL

Shortlisted Writers' News 'Unlikely Couple' Competition 2011

The café was in the better end of town and deserted. Breakfast (more croissant than fry-up) had finished and the morning coffee ladies (gossiping, whilst their husbands brokered mortgages for those unable to pay) had yet to arrive.

Steve took a table in the corner, away from the window. Julia had emphasised that this meeting was confidential. She had a business proposition for him and the fewer people that knew about it, the better.

He'd worn a suit to impress her. It had come from EBay two years earlier, for his school prom, and this morning he'd sneaked a plain blue tie from his father's wardrobe. The get-up felt suffocating and Steve loosened the knot at his neck and then took the jacket off. As he did so he caught the gentle perfume that still lingered on the fabric and a raunchy image galloped into his mind. He'd come of age on that prom night. Since then the same success with any other girl had eluded him but with Helen he was getting near.

When Julia had phoned to arrange this meeting he'd almost dropped his mobile with shock. It was no secret that Julia hated him. He'd asked her if Helen would be coming too, assuming that his girlfriend would be privy to whatever her mother was going to propose.

"No," Julia said brusquely, "she'll be in the middle of her Philosophy AS exam. Or had you forgotten that the girl you profess to love is still at school and aiming to read Politics, Philosophy and Economics at Oxbridge?"

The acid tone of her voice astounded him but the remark was in line with Julia's constant attempts to belittle him.

"Delivering potatoes is like being an undertaker or a hairdresser," she'd said on first hearing about Steve's job.

"How do you mean?" he'd asked, wrong footed by this too thin, overly made-up woman.

"People will always die, always need their hair cutting and they'll always need their potatoes delivering. It's hardly a career though, is it?"

Steve wanted to say that Julia's post of lecturer in childcare at the local college was hardly on a par with Bill Gates or Richard Branson. For the sake of his relationship with her daughter he kept his mouth shut but the longer he went out with Helen, the harder it was to put up with Julia's attitude towards him.

If he and Helen went upstairs to talk in private,

listen to music or maybe have a kiss and a cuddle, Julia would stalk the landing. She would constantly knock on the door offering cups of tea or suggesting they came downstairs to watch TV. Sometimes she flung the door open unannounced.

"She doesn't trust me. She thinks I'm going to take advantage of you," Steve complained to Helen.

"It's not that," Helen always defended her mother. "She has high hopes of her only child. She doesn't want me to be pregnant at 19 like her – so she's over protective."

"And you're over the age of consent and I'm always over prepared. Despite what your mother might think - I don't want to make a baby either."

Helen had flushed at this last remark and Steve had kicked himself. Helen was special and if he rushed her then he might lose her altogether.

Steve raised his hand to attract Julia's attention as she walked into the café, although it was hardly necessary amongst all the empty tables.

"Have you ordered?" she asked.

"No, I was waiting for you."

"So you didn't have to open your wallet," Julia muttered under her breath but Steve caught the words.

"I wanted to treat you," he lied quickly. "Do you fancy some cake as well as a coffee?"

It was a calculated gamble - he couldn't afford gateaux as well as drinks. He was banking on Julia still being on her permanent diet and refusing anything other than salad.

"How kind!" she flashed him an empty smile and picked up the menu.

Steve went cold – not having enough money

would be the ultimate humiliation. Worse than that time Julia opened the bedroom door and caught them in full snog.

A waitress hovered. Steve debated ordering a glass of orange squash because it was the cheapest thing listed but that would look odd in front of a woman who knew he was a caffeine addict.

He remembered his manners and indicated that Julia should go first. Then he dug into his jacket pocket hoping to discover some forgotten coins – maybe the change from a round of drinks at the prom. But the cupboard was bare.

"The cakes look lovely," Julia said and then moved her lips into a meaningless curve again. "But I'm watching my figure so I'll just have an unsweetened lemon tea, please."

Steve relaxed a little. "I'd like a small filter coffee, thank you."

Julia leaned towards him and lowered her voice when the waitress had left.

"I have a proposition for you. Call it a business deal. I pay you for doing a service for me."

Steve stared at her, not comprehending.

"It's to do with Helen," she continued. "I want you to break off the relationship."

"What!"

"The next 12 months are vital if she is to get a place at Oxford or Cambridge. She doesn't need the distraction of a boyfriend."

"Are we talking about any boyfriend or me in particular?"

Anger was budding within him at this controlling, snobbish woman.

"Well ..."

That pause, as Julia searched unsuccessfully for an answer, told him everything. A richer, better educated, more well-to-do boy would be perfectly acceptable for her beloved daughter - whether there were exams to sit or not.

"You said you would pay me," Steve prompted.

He had no intention of accepting a few pounds in exchange for giving up Helen; she was the only one who believed he could do better than van driving. But he may as well let Julia show her true colours so that he could tell Helen exactly what her cow of a mother was like.

"Ten ... thousand ... pounds," she said the words slowly and emphatically.

Steve swallowed. She was talking real money. It was enough to upgrade his white van and help finance his market garden dream.

"But for that I would need you to sign a contract in the presence of my solicitor. If you break the contract then every penny would have to be paid back immediately."

Steve wondered if such a contract was enforceable - but Julia was too efficient not to have checked it out first.

"It takes two to tango," he said. "By offering me this money you are implying that your daughter finds me irresistible and wouldn't end the relationship of her own accord."

"Helen is too young to know what's best for her. I've done research and written academic papers on dysfunctional families as part of my job. Any grandchild of mine will have an educated man for a father. As I tell my students, the saying 'like father, like son' is founded heavily in truth."

"What about the government's plan for social mobility?"

Julia ignored his remark.

"Write a letter to Helen telling her that it's all over. Here, I brought notepaper and a pen with me."

Steve stared at the proffered fountain pen and heavy cream notepaper.

"Helen knows I don't own paper like that or a proper ink pen. She'll realise the letter isn't genuine."

At that moment the waitress appeared with their drinks.

"Would it be possible for my companion to have a page from your notebook and loan of your biro for a few minutes?" Julia asked the girl.

Steve picked up the borrowed pen and then put it down again.

"I need time to think," he said.

"You have ten minutes." Julia buried herself in a glossy magazine.

Helen was special. Yes, she was one of the fittest girls he knew but there was more to Helen than the physical stuff. She wasn't a heavily made-up, straightened hair, mini-skirted clone of the girls on his council estate. Helen talked about what they saw on the news and cared about things happening in countries he'd never heard of. She didn't laugh at his dream of running a market garden and had got him a load of leaflets about college courses – courses that could become a reality if he had £10,000.

"Five minutes."

But she'd probably find some other swanky boyfriend when she went to Uni and he'd lose her anyway. The money would give him a fair stab at the future.

***

"Am I glad that is over?!"

"I will so never sit another Philosophy exam – that subject is dropped as of now!"

"Mum! Steve! What are you two doing here?"

The two heads at the corner table jerked towards the group of teenaged girls that had just hurtled into the cafe.

"Helen!" the pair proclaimed in startled unison.

Helen stared at them. There appeared to be some sort of illicit pact between her mother and her boyfriend – they looked guilty as hell. She prayed that this wasn't the sort of dirty affair that got splashed across the front of the cheap women's weeklies.

Steve dropped his eyes and started scribbling something. Then he stood up abruptly, causing his chair to crash to the ground behind him.

"I've written it," he murmured.

"Give it to her on your way out. I'll be in touch about the rest."

"What's going on?" Helen asked as Steve strode towards her.

Without looking at her he pushed a folded piece of paper into her hand and then walked out on to the street.

Helen unfolded the note.

"I love you more than all the riches in the world. Call you later. XXXXX."

***

From outside the window Steve saw Helen smile with

pleasure at his words. She looked up and caught his eye. It had been tempting to explain in the note what a bitch her mother was but that would've brought Helen's world tumbling down. He loved her too much to do that.

OUT OF THE SHADOWS

Shortlisted 5 Minute Fiction 'Valentine Story' Competition 2012

Sylvia had been out with married men many times before. They promised the earth but rarely delivered and, no matter how many times they voiced their intentions, married men never left their wives. They left Sylvia instead, stealing her confidence and self-worth. All she could do was wipe the tears, put on more lipstick and start all over again.

But Gerald was different.

Right now he was dissolving vows to end a twenty year commitment. In half an hour he would be here, starting a new life with her. He wouldn't let her down at the last minute like so many others, 'for the sake of the children'.

Like all her lovers, she'd found out that Gerald was spoken for after she'd become enamoured with him. But being with Gerald was different – they hadn't even consummated their relationship yet. He was the only man who'd valued her as a person and not a sex toy.

She'd met him at adult swimming lessons and they'd got chatting over powdery hot chocolate from a temperamental machine. Unusually for his age, Gerald had no paunch and he had the kindest of dark brown eyes and wasn't wearing a wedding ring. This wasn't absolute proof that there was no wife but his creased shirts and the microwave meal for one, half-hidden beneath the towel in his bag, led her to this assumption.

To start with he'd been aloof and hadn't responded to her wide-eyed flirtatious remarks or her new up-lifting bikini. Then they'd discovered their common need for a hot, wet blood sugar boost after all that exertion in the water. She'd asked him back for coffee after the third lesson and he'd seemed almost pathetically grateful for the invitation.

In the hope of relaxing him enough to take things a step further (which was the only way Sylvia knew of hooking a guy), she'd put a bottle of brandy on the tray with the mugs and Penguin biscuits. But Gerald had turned down the alcohol and carefully removed her hand each time it found its way onto his knee or up to the neck of his shirt.

"I'm sorry, Sylvia," he'd said. "You're a lovely lady but at the moment I can only offer friendship."

It was a slap in the face. Even though Sylvia was used to rejection she usually got past first base. After he'd gone, she examined her naked body in the full length mirror. Post-50 everything had started to droop but the swimming was toning up her thighs and stomach nicely. For a woman of her age, she had a good figure.

The next week Gerald had brought flowers with a note of apology. Since then, Sylvia was proud to say, they'd built a relationship based on mutual respect with nothing more physical than a peck on the cheek when they parted.

Once they'd become relaxed in each other's company, Gerald had made the shocking confession.

"I've never slept with a woman." He came out with it just like that, apropos of nothing. "If I'm ever free to move our relationship forward, will you do me the honour of taking my virginity?"

Then he'd told her about his current set-up.

"I give, give, give constantly and get nothing back. Attending social events alone is one of the worst things. I'm good at circulating and small-talk is my specialty. But if I stop the forced bonhomie and stand still for a second then I'm on my own. I want a friendly face at my side, someone who wants me for myself and not what I represent."

"When you're free, I'll accompany you to the ends of the earth," Sylvia told him. In Gerald she'd finally found someone precious, someone who wasn't just interested in the physical side of an affair.

***

He'd felt much better after confessing all to Sylvia.

Being a woman of a certain age, he'd thought she would be content with just a platonic friendship. But every week her body language had told him that she craved physical intimacy - something he hadn't been free to give.

At first he'd been immune to her best assets, even in the pool, where not much was left to the imagination. It must have been the result of all those years of self-denial.

He'd never been attracted to his parishioners in a sexual way and was always aghast when he read of colleagues breaking their vow of chastity. He felt, that with a certain amount of self-discipline and ingrained habit, it was possible to lead a life without sex - especially if you'd never experienced the pleasures of the flesh before coming into the church.

So feeling the first stirrings of something other than friendship for Sylvia had been both an enjoyable and shocking surprise.

But he wasn't giving up the church for sex alone. Sylvia had much more to offer than that. She was a cure for the dark pool of loneliness that nestled deep within.

Every day he listened to the staff in the church office talk fondly about their children and spouses. He would smile and nod but could add nothing to their conversation because he always went home to an empty house.

Sylvia, with her warm chatter, was making him light-hearted in a way that had been missing since he first took his vows. She was a safety valve when he was weighed down by the woes of parishioners or frustrated by instructions from higher up the clergy tree.

And now, the cassock and dog-collar discarded, he was going to start over in the arms and ample bosom of this good woman.

Sylvia's house was full of noise and strangers when he arrived. Terrified, he wanted to turn and run but she'd already seen him. He plastered on his parish smile and slipped into the small-talk circulating mode he thought he'd left behind.

Then she was at his side, kissing him publicly and passionately on the lips. The unknown people cheered.

"I hope you don't mind," she whispered. "I organised a 'Starting Over' party. I'm finished with relationships conducted in the shadows – we are going to love each other in the sunlight."

Without hesitation, he kissed her back.

CONSEQUENCES

Winner Freelance Market News Short Story 'I didn't want to …' Competition September 2009

I didn't want to go to the press but what else could I do?

Judith Carter had just been appointed the new 'Minister for the Family'. She had taken the platform at the Party conference in a blaze of flash bulbs and rousing music and had outlined her plans for bringing 'hard-working families' back to the centre of the political agenda.

"There will be a return to tax incentives for married couples," she'd proclaimed in her strident voice. "Plus an increased tax allowance for families where one parent chooses to stay at home and look after the children."

I watched all this on television with my two-month-old daughter at my breast. During the standing ovation that followed there were shots of the cheering audience with clapping hands raised above their heads.

The camera rested momentarily on a familiar face – George, my husband. He was stamping his feet and mouthing words that no microphone could pick up. To me it was obvious that he was basking in Judith's reflected glory; he had every right to – he is her speech writer. But I had never seen him that proud before and I felt like a knife was slicing through my heart.

"The party is in love," said the presenter back in the studio, "with this vibrant newcomer who is doing what the grass-roots members have demanded for so long."

That's when I decided someone had to take the moral high ground. I couldn't let people put their trust in this woman whose personal belief in the importance of family was non-existent.

George and I have been together since university. I supported us both with my teacher's salary when he earned a pittance as a political researcher. Judith Carter was a colleague of mine. Then she became an MP and rose rapidly through the ranks.

Just before I got pregnant I sounded her out about an opportunity for George. As a result he got his current post and we could finally afford to start a family. He loves this new job even though his long hours mean we don't see much of each other. I was prepared to put up with it until he started coming home smelling of someone else's perfume.

"Honestly Ann! Judith and I work closely together." His sudden flush made him look as guilty as hell. "If we're staring at the same lap-top screen then maybe her scent wafts over."

Yesterday I received the private detective's report and it states categorically that George Beams and Judith Carter have a 'close relationship'.

She's kicked me in the teeth so I'm going to do the same to her.

The picture will appear in tomorrow's paper and my fee goes to charity. I made sure that the newspaper indicated this in print; I want the public to know that they should be questioning the morality of the Family Minister not the financial motivation of the anonymous person supplying the picture.

***

I didn't want to believe the newspaper picture that had been pushed in front of me. It didn't show my standing ovation as Minister for the Family instead it was from a past life that I had all but forgotten about.

"We have to get a comment to the press quickly," said Paul, my constituency secretary. "Otherwise you'll be the shortest serving Family Minister in history."

"It was fifteen years ago, Paul. I wasn't even an MP – how is it relevant now?"

The picture was slightly blurred but my face was immediately recognisable. I was wearing a low-cut T-shirt with the words 'HEN' emblazoned across it and a mini skirt made of 'L' plates. I had one knee raised provocatively, with my foot resting on a scruffy staff-room armchair and revealing too much thigh and suspender. But it had been a photo taken amongst friends.

I'd been touched that my female teaching

colleagues had gone to the trouble of getting me all dressed up for my hen-night. I'd made a token protest when they produced the fishnets and 'L' plates but after a couple of glasses of wine I'd been happy to oblige.

"Everyone has a hen night don't they?"

"Not like yours." Paul jabbed his finger at the scantily-clad, good-looking male casually stroking my knee.

"He's only a strip-a-gram." I tried to keep my voice casual but my heart began to pound.

"The handsome young strip-a-gram was in Carter's Sixth form Economics group." Paul read aloud from the paper. "Is this appropriate behaviour between a teacher and pupil? Would you trust your son with our new Minister for the Family?"

I started to tremble. There had been no inappropriate behaviour that evening. James had rested his hand on my thigh for the photo. Then he'd been paid and gone home to his A' level revision whilst we'd had a night on the town.

"It was a business arrangement. He and his friend had set themselves up as odd job men to save for a gap year. They did whatever you asked – car washing, lawn mowing, window cleaning. The strip-a-gram was Ann's idea …"

I put my hand to my mouth. George had told me that Ann had some weird suspicions about an affair – was this her sick way of getting revenge? Revenge for something that could never happen between me and any man since my short-lived marriage.

"Why would somebody stab you in the back like this?" Paul was agitated now. "It wasn't for money; that went to charity. It wouldn't be Ann, she'd be putting George's job with you on the line. It must be the boy in the picture. What's his name?"

"James Hardcastle." Somehow his name had stuck in my mind after all those years. "But he was sweet. He'd never do anything like this."

Paul threw me a funny look. "I'm going to Google him."

"He was just a nervous 17-year-old."

"Look." Paul tilted the computer screen towards me. "He's a priest now. People should be warned."

***

"I didn't want to do it." I tried to explain as the churchwarden waved the tabloid in front of me.

"Minister's Teenage Kiss-a-gram Named!" shouted the headline.

"You look like you were enjoying yourself to me, Vicar." He stared at the photo again.

I couldn't admit to my churchwarden how extremely flattered I'd been at 17-years-old when asked to show off my body to one of the best looking teachers in the school.

"So how do I explain this to the parishioners? The Mothers' Union are terribly disappointed. They want to bring in the Bishop."

They did and I took the call from him in my study later that afternoon.

"It was boyish high jinks," I explained as soon as he mentioned the newspaper story. "If it was one of our choir boys we'd advise him of the error of his ways but we wouldn't dismiss him."

"I agree." The Bishop's voice was as hard as stone. "But you're not a choir boy and it's not just the

Mothers' Union. I've had a phone call from the Minister's secretary, Paul Carter. He says you sent that photo to the press."

"Me?" My blood ran cold.

"And he's suggesting you are not a suitable role model for young people and could be a danger to them."

My career was about to go up in smoke. These were serious allegations.

"I swear it wasn't me. After that night I finished my A' levels and never saw any of the teachers again. I'd never even seen that photo until it was in the paper."

"I've persuaded Mr Carter to give us 24 hours before he publicly demands that the church takes disciplinary action. I will consult our lawyers and I suggest you start to build your defence."

Mrs Beams, one of the teachers, had taken photos that night. It had been her idea that I should touch the soon-to-be Mrs Carter's thigh. My hand had been shaking and they'd both laughed. I'd been the only sober one there. If it was Mrs Beams' camera then they must be her photos.

I phoned the newspaper but they refused to break their confidentiality agreement. They wouldn't even call the bishop and say it wasn't me who had supplied the picture.

Google lead me to Mrs Beams' front door. She answered with an infant in her arms and a sudden fearful recognition in her eyes.

"My career's in ruins," I said.

"She was stealing my husband! I did it for my daughter!"

"I hope you're satisfied." A man barged between

us on his way into the house. "Judith's out of the cabinet and I'm out of a job."

Someone else appeared and pushed a brown envelope at Mrs Beams.

"A revised report," he panted. "My assistant jumped the gun. There was no affair. Carter's a les…"

He paused at the sight of the white band at my neck.

"…she has other inclinations," he finished lamely and left.

Mrs Beams face contorted with anguish. "I didn't want to…"

A TANGLED WEB

Runner-up in the 2008 Galaxy Ripple/Company/Little Black Dress Short Story Competition

Susie's heart thumped and her mouth went dry as the plane descended into Prague airport.

She rehearsed her excuse one last time.

"Kerry, we're both really sorry but Marcus can't make your wedding."

Misleading her younger sister in an email hadn't seemed to matter but lying to her in person was against Susie's usual principles.

"His brother's getting married on the same day, so that has to take priority."

It sounded too coincidental. Maybe she should try the truth. She whispered it to herself.

"Kerry, Marcus won't be at your wedding because he doesn't exist."

"Sorry, I didn't quite catch what you said."

Susie jumped and stared at the man on her left, who was looking at her questioningly. Until now he'd been hidden behind a newspaper.

"I was talking to myself." A flush spread, like spilt wine, over her cheeks, making her feel even more foolish.

"Then I'll pretend I didn't notice." He seemed to be struggling to suppress a grin but it escaped through his twinkling brown eyes. "I'm James, by the way."

He offered her a large, firm hand which held hers slightly longer than necessary.

Susie felt shaky. James was Marcus incarnate; with broad shoulders, thick dark hair and a delicious smile.

She hadn't planned to invent a boyfriend. It had started with her younger sister's emails.

Hi Susie!
Prague is a cool place to study! It's overrun with fit students, including Paul & we're getting serious! Stop pining over Graham!
Love Kerry xxxx

Each message was peppered with exclamation marks and smiley face icons. Susie knew her replies were boring but after splitting with Graham she was relishing time on her own to get her new flat in order.

Dear Kerry,
Marcus from downstairs has put shelves up for me. I made him dinner in return.
Love Susie.

Susie!
Paul proposed on Charles Bridge! How's the big

romance with Marcus! Glad you're over gormless Graham.
Luv Kerry (and Paul!) xxxxxx

It was easier to let Kerry think that she had a new man than explain that Marcus was actually 50 and gay and that she was still single. Susie didn't want anyone feeling sorry for her spinsterish situation. So, she began to elaborate.

Hi Kerry,
I've known Marcus 6 months and we're spending more and more time together…
Love Susie.

The plane bumped onto the runway and the brakes roared into action.

"I hate that bit," said James.

They stood together at the baggage carousel and James manhandled her suitcase from the conveyor belt.

"What about your luggage?" she asked, as they walked towards the Customs hall.

"I travel light." He indicated the rucksack that he'd taken on the plane as hand luggage. "I'm doing my bit for the environment."

Susie blushed as she thought of the 4 pairs of shoes, hairdryer and straighteners she'd packed for the weekend. When she came over for the wedding in a month's time she'd need at least 2 suitcases.

The 'Nothing to Declare' queue swallowed them up and spat them out separately.

Kerry pounced on Susie in Arrivals with a bear hug.

"It's great to see you. The dress fitting is booked for this afternoon – yours is fantastic!"

Susie broke free from her exuberant sister.

"On the plane I met this really handsome…"

Then she remembered she was supposed to be in love with Marcus. But Kerry hadn't heard, she was busy scanning the crowd still emerging from the customs hall.

"James! Over here!"

Kerry was waving like a windmill at the man from the plane.

"Susie, this is James. He's Paul's best man. James this is Susie, my sister and bridesmaid."

"We've met."

But James held his hand out in greeting again and Susie took it eagerly.

Kerry shepherded them both into a taxi and Susie knew she had to get this lie out of the way or it would eat her up and spoil the rest of the weekend.

"Marcus can't make the wedding," she blurted out as soon as they'd left the airport perimeter. "His brother's getting married on the same day."

She carried on babbling, unable to look her sister in the eye.

"Blood's thicker than water and all that. So he'll be going there. Any other weekend would've been fine – it's just bad luck."

Susie flopped back into the taxi seat, feeling as limp as a lettuce now that the worst was over.

"That's great," said Kerry.

"You mean you didn't want him?" Susie couldn't believe how defensive she felt over someone who didn't exist.

"No! I can't wait to meet him. But we've had to

postpone the wedding for a week so that Paul's uncle from Australia can make it. So your Marcus can come after all!"

"Oh no! I mean fantastic, he'll be so pleased."

Susie's mind whirled as her excuse disintegrated before her eyes. Then, she caught James glancing at her with a knowing look.

He must have heard her furtive whisperings in the air. She gave him a weak smile and hoped he could be trusted.

The dress fitting reminded Susie of childhood princess games. A flight of narrow stairs led to a dumpy but jolly, Czech fairy godmother, who had sewn a gold sheath dress to Susie's emailed measurements and it fitted perfectly. The gown even made her forget that she was a frumpy spinster playing bridesmaid to her younger sister. All that work on the cross-trainer in the gym had been worth it, just a shame that there wasn't a real live Marcus to admire her curves in this dress…

Kerry's wedding dress was exquisite. When she tried the veil Susie felt the beginnings of tears at the back of her eyes as she admired her sister in the cream silk and lace creation.

"You must have the dumplings and a beer," Kerry ordered her sister and James later that evening. "It's the local speciality."

The four of them were studying the menu in a tiny restaurant hidden in the maze of Prague streets.

Susie began to feel a warm glow as they ate and chatted by the light of a flickering candle. She usually drank wine but the light Czech beer slipped down easily. Susie found herself flirting with James and forgetting all about imaginary Marcus and the need to invent a new reason why he wouldn't be at the wedding.

"You do know that the best man and the bridesmaid have to share at least one slow dance?" James softly reminded her and touched her hand.

The bolt of electricity between them startled Susie.

"Careful you two," cautioned Kerry. "Susie's spoken for. I don't want any scenes at my wedding when the bridesmaid's boyfriend discovers he has a love rival, our best man!"

Kerry was laughing but Susie suddenly sobered up and declared she was ready for bed. In that convivial atmosphere it would have been impossible to stay faithful to non-existent Marcus even if she had wanted to – and she definitely didn't want to!

Kerry and Paul took their guests to the Pinkas Synagogue the following morning. The solemnity of the tragedy displayed there silenced the foursome. They walked through the small museum and gazed at the names of the thousands of Jews killed at the hands of the Nazis.

"It's criminal for us to waste one moment of our lives when so many had theirs brutally cut short," James whispered to Susie.

Susie swallowed the lump in her throat. She didn't even know any of these people so why did she want to cry? Susie blew her nose and smiled weakly at James.

"Hey, don't let this spoil your weekend away." He brushed some hair from her face. "Your Marcus is a very lucky man."

Susie felt James stare right into her soul and see the truth behind the lies. She said nothing; whatever she said about the non-existence of Marcus would make her look idiotic. Instead she would have to let the possibility of romance with James pass her by.

They left the names behind and moved onto a display of children's art.

"These pictures are drawn by the youngsters in concentration camps," explained Kerry.

Susie sniffed and thought of the seven-year-olds that she taught back home. They had their moments of mischief and naughtiness but essentially, like all young children, they were innocent of any crime and deserved to be treated well.

She felt James' warm, firm hand in hers and she squeezed it gratefully.

They blinked back out into the sunshine and found a pavement café.

"You must bring Marcus here one day," said Paul.

Susie stared into her iced coffee to avoid meeting James' knowing eyes.

"Kerry's told me so much about him that he already seems like family."

Susie felt James staring at her again, as though he was willing her to speak the truth.

"Let's ask him to be an usher!" suggested Kerry, suddenly. "He and Susie are so close that he's almost my brother-in-law anyway. He ought to be involved."

"No!" Susie almost shouted. "You can't, you've never even met him."

"I trust your good taste, big sister. I've liked all your boyfriends except Jonathan with the owl-like glasses, he used to pull my pig-tails when you weren't looking."

Susie felt her cheeks redden as James snorted with laughter.

"Text Marcus now and ask him to be our usher," ordered Kerry. "If you won't, I will."

She reached for her sister's phone.

"I'll do it."

She couldn't risk Kerry going through her phonebook and texting gay Marcus in the flat below. Susie pushed random keys and sent an imaginary text.

"The next stop on our itinerary is Charles Bridge," announced Kerry when she was sure the text had been sent.

"And tell me when Marcus replies," she added.

The bridge was crowded with tourists and Kerry played at tour guide, reading out the history of each statue as they slowly went over the bridge.

"This is St. John of Nepomuk. The story goes that King Wencelas had him thrown off the bridge because he refused to reveal the secrets confessed to him by Wencelas' wife. If you touch the lady on the right of the statue then you will return to Prague and if you make a wish whilst touching the dog on the left then it will come true."

"Come on, let's make a wish," said James guiding Susie towards the statue.

Susie tried to formulate a wish to solve the web of deceit she'd entangled herself in.

"Ladies first."

Susie placed her hand on the statue and silently wished for her make-believe relationship with Marcus to be replaced with the reality of romance with James.

Then she waited and wondered whilst James placed his hand where hers had been. After a few seconds he turned back towards her.

"For my wish to come true you have to tell Kerry the truth about Marcus."

Susie's heart sang with the realisation that James' wish matched hers. But she couldn't speak.

"Or do I do like King Wencelas and throw you into the river?" James' mouth was smiling but his eyes were deadly serious.

He slipped his hand into hers. "Don't let life pass you by, Susie."

She squeezed his hand and thought of those child artists who hadn't even had a chance at life. She owed it to them to make the most of hers.

Kerry looked up from her guidebook as Susie and James approached.

"Kerry," Susie began. "I haven't been entirely truthful about Marcus."

She paused, the shame of misleading her sister reddening her cheeks.

"I don't have a boyfriend called Marcus. I made him up because I got fed up of people feeling sorry for me after I split with Graham."

"You silly thing…." began Kerry affectionately.

James silenced her with his hand and put an arm around Susie's waist.

"So there'll be no problem with the bridesmaid and best man sharing slow dances at your wedding."

Then Susie was swept into an embrace with a very real man.

Old Friends

SALLY JENKINS

CONTENTS

ANOTHER FINE MESS

Diana grabbed the shrieking phone as she hunted for her car keys, handed out dinner money and hastily salvaged a dirty sock from behind the front door.

"Ah, Diana? It's Tim Mason from Sparkling Clean Homes - Revisited. Just to let you know we've changed the shooting schedule, and we need to film our return visit this afternoon, about five thirty."

Diana's knees felt distinctly wobbly as she stared in panic at the dust on the telephone shelf, the jumble of shoes and bags under the stairs and the beginnings of a cobweb by the front door. Only six months ago, the hit squad from the popular makeover programme had left her house gleaming - and now it was back to its previous grubby, cluttered muddle.

"It will only take about an hour," Tim was saying soothingly. "Just so that you can show us whether you've managed to stick to our cleaning regime, and tell us if the original programme helped you get on top of things. OK? There's no need to go to any great effort - remember it's your home and not a film set."

"That's fine." It sounded to Diana as if someone else was uttering her words as she remembered just how sticky the kitchen floor was - and that, horrors! She hadn't actually pulled the settee out since the camera crew had been there last.

"It would be good if you could have a meal in the oven," continued Tim airily. "Then we can show you serving it to the family as the final credits roll."

She stared around in utter shame at the state of her house. Even though the children were in their teens, being a working mother didn't get any easier - and the original visit by the Sparkling Clean Homes crew had worked absolute wonders, successfully shifting years of accumulated clutter, dust and dirty finger marks.

But since then, she'd been drafted on to the PTA, persuaded to help out with Amy's Guide Company and promoted at work - little wonder that she never had any time for things like housework or cooking.

Glancing at her watch, she stuffed a pile of magazines under a chair cushion, bundled a basket of un-ironed washing into a dark corner and dusted the television with her palm. It wasn't nearly enough.

She dashed into the bathroom to put out clean towels. A bottle of expensive shampoo was disgorging thick yellow goo on to the bath mat, a heap of muddy socks was festering on the floor near the dirty linen basket and there was a distinct grey tideline around the bath.

An image of a television advert suddenly flashed through her mind - the one in which a teenager surveys a house full of illicit party debris, with his parents' return imminent. Hmmmm - what worked for him, just might work for her too.

In desperation she grabbed the Yellow Pages and left for work.

Two minutes later she was back, furtively trying to hide a house key under the mud-encrusted doormat.

Once at the office, Diana attempted to let her fingers do the walking. It quickly turned into a high hurdles race.

"It's just a one-off clean that I need."

But A1 Domestics were only interested in regular contracts.

"Yes, it does have to be today."

But Elbow Power was fully booked up until the following week.

"No, I'm not sure whether I've got any bleach and the Hoover's temperamental."

But Supa Clean wouldn't provide any cleaning materials.

"Fantastic! Thanks so much. The key's under the mat."

Zippy Maids had solved the problem and promised to be finished by three o'clock. Diana's shoulders drooped with relief as she put the phone down.

"You really shouldn't do that, you know, Diana."

She stared questioningly at her ear-wigging boss, Paul. Surely he wasn't going to preach about a woman's place being in the home and that hiring a cleaner was nothing short of selling one's soul to the devil. He couldn't do that, not after finally promoting her to project leader.

"Leaving your key under the mat," he explained. "The house will be stripped bare when you get home - either that or there'll be some mad, axe-wielding psychopath hiding under your bed."

Diana spent the day worrying about the key being used by a burglar and invalidating the house insurance. She couldn't decide which was worse - total humiliation on national television as her slovenly housekeeping was beamed into millions of homes, or the possibility of an anonymous furniture van driving away with all their dusty, sticky worldly goods with no recompense forthcoming from the insurance company.

Her stomach lurched as she suddenly remembered Tim's request for a meal in the oven. There was only the kids' favourite hot and spicy pizza lurking in the fridge. That would not look good on camera.

Mentally, Diana went through her freezer contents - ice cream Mars bars, chips and half a box of vegetarian sausages (left over from Amy's very short meat-free phase).

There was no alternative but to dash to the supermarket and hope to find something that looked home-made. Paul frowned as she asked whether she could leave the office half an hour early.

"I need my 15 minutes of fame to at least show me as an average housewife rather than a disgraceful one," Diana pleaded.

Everyone and his dog, it seemed, were congregated in the supermarket's Ready Meals aisle. What was wrong with people these days - didn't anyone cook for themselves anymore?

She needed something that looked home-made

and wholesome. Diana manoeuvred the trolley past Chinese, Indian, Thai and Italian. That left her with a choice between shepherd's pie, fish pie or individual portions of roast beef and Yorkshire pudding.

The shepherd's pie looked the most home-made and she picked one that looked slightly burnt, deciding it would appear more realistic on camera. Grabbing a bag of frozen carrots and an apple crumble, she added a tin of custard as an afterthought.

There should be plenty of time to get her purchases out of their cartons and into her own dishes before the film crew arrived. Diana's mobile beeped as she hurried through the checkout.

"Mum!" Amy's voice was anxious. "You will be at my netball match, won't you?"

Diana swore silently to herself for forgetting about Amy's first game as team captain. Would it really matter so much if the film crew saw her arriving home with a shop-bought shepherd's pie instead of thinking she'd spent the afternoon chopping, frying and mashing? Surely they wouldn't betray her and the spirit of their own show in front of the viewers?

"I'm on my way now, love."

An hour later Diana proudly drove the victorious captain into their cul-de-sac - and her heart froze. She pulled in and climbed out of the car with legs of lead.

The Zippy Maids van was still there. Worse, the television production company's van was parked behind it and there appeared to be a fairly heated argument in progress on her driveway, between a white-coated lady and the show's producer, Tim Mason.

"It's too clean," Tim was protesting. "Our

viewers won't believe that a working woman with two teenagers can keep her house looking like a showhome."

The woman folded her arms. "I'm being paid to do a job and Zippy Maids has a reputation to maintain."

"I just need to scatter some magazines, put a couple of mugs and plates on the draining board and maybe a pair of jeans on the boy's bed - oh, and some muddy football boots in the utility room."

"Over my dead body."

Diana pushed Amy through the front door with whispered instructions to put the supermarket food into casserole dishes ready to put into the oven.

"It's too late for us to get started now. I'll have to come back another day," Tim said abruptly to Diana on his way back to the van. "This is a reality show, not a shoot for Perfect Homes magazine. Get yourself a less thorough cleaner next time."

As Diana waved off an irate Zippy Maid and a frustrated film crew, the sound of crashing glass reached her from the kitchen.

Her sparkling kitchen floor was slowly disappearing beneath an oozing shepherd's pie and a broken casserole dish.

"I'm sorry, Mum," Amy groaned.

"Don't worry." Diana relaxed for the first time that day. "Give me a hug. I tell you what. When your brother gets in, let's have hot and spicy pizza followed by ice cream Mars bars, in front of the TV. That producer was absolutely right; this is our home - not a film set."

PLEASE HOLD!

"Please enter your sort code followed by the hash key."

Tap, tap, tap.

"Please enter your account code followed by the hash key."

Tap, tap, tap.

"Please hold to speak to a customer adviser."

I accompanied the muzak with finger drumming on the telephone shelf.

"Good morning, my name is Tracey. Please can I have your date of birth?"

"Thirteenth of March, 1960."

"And your mother's maiden name?"

"Hartley."

"And how may I help you to…"

There was a sharp click, the phone emitted a high pitched beep and then went silent. I emitted words not usually in my vocabulary. My fist made satisfying contact with the shelf and the Present from Barmouth message pad danced a jig.

That had been my second frustrating phone call within half an hour; the first had been Tom on his mobile from university.

"Mum? I need money."

"Hi, Tom. What for?"

"Text books for the course."

I could clearly hear feminine giggles.

"How much?"

"Sixty? Today, if possible."

"Well…"

"Thanks, Mum." And he was gone.

It's hard to refuse your child when he's a hundred miles from home and surviving on baked beans in second-rate accommodation whilst studying late into the night. I knew I should withhold the money in order to teach him how to budget. But his baby picture is on the wall near the phone and he looks so angelic, lying naked on a fur rug and kicking his chubby soft legs.

I could have transferred the money to Tom using the internet instead of the phone. He's shown me how, loads of times. But somehow I don't quite trust it; there's so much talk of hackers and identity theft.

Anyway, after the bank cut me off I couldn't face all that tapping of numbers and wallpaper music again so I decided to ring Tom back and tell him he'd have to wait another day for the books.

"Tom? It's me again."

"Was that my phone?" His words were almost drowned by rustling and laughing.

"It's OK. The screen said it was your mum so I

switched it off." It was the voice of the giggling girl from earlier.

"Thanks. She'll just be confirming the money transfer. She doesn't do texting. Says it's nicer to hear someone's voice. Anyway, that means I can afford to get my round in now. Shall we have doubles?"

I should have hung up but I couldn't. I was paralysed by what I was hearing.

"Your mum is good. Mine asks for receipts to show what I've spent the money on. No way could I spend text book money on concert tickets. It's a fabulous birthday treat. Thanks."

"Let's drink to Tom's mum!" suggested a male voice. "Long may her wonderful generosity continue!"

Seething, I ended the call and stared at Tom's photo. What I'd just heard had changed the innocent baby into someone I didn't quite trust. I could no longer picture him toiling away in a lonely bedroom surrounded by an ever growing pile of books and empty coffee mugs. It was time to put some mutual respect back into our relationship.

He phoned again three days later.

"Mum, the money's not arrived." He was straight to the point and sounded agitated. "They'll sell out if I'm not quick. Could you drive down with the cash?"

"Please enter your sort code followed by the hash key."

"What? I could fail if I don't have these books."

"Please enter your account number followed by the hash key."

"What's with the funny voice, Mum?"

"Please hold to speak to a customer adviser."

I hummed Edelweiss down the phone to my

increasingly irate son.

"Good morning my name is Joyce. Please can I have your date of birth?"

In a slightly stunned voice Tom gave the information.

"And your maiden's name?"

"What do you mean?"

"That giggly girlfriend of yours."

"Sophie. What is this, Mum, the Spanish Inquisition?"

"I'm sorry this bank only funds serious academic endeavour. Not birthday outings for maidens."

I put the phone down.

POINTS MEAN PRIZES

Lesley had to act quickly. She wanted to be out of the house before Robert returned. She shoved the note under the box of teabags, where he couldn't miss it.

The sight of that box, with its patchwork of holes, reinforced her determination to make Robert choose - before it was even finished he'd cut tokens from the cardboard to send for a mug emblazoned with tea-drinking chimpanzees.

"Mum! Are you ready?"

Lesley threw on her coat, grabbed her suitcase and joined her daughter in the car.

"How do you think Dad'll take it?" Jenny asked anxiously as she reversed out of the drive.

Lesley imagined her husband coming back from the supermarket to an empty house. There'd be no one there to listen to his tales of having gained so many extra loyalty points for buying expensive yoghurt or cereal multi-packs that they were never likely to eat.

"I don't know but I just can't go on living under his regime of tokens and loyalty cards. There is no free choice in our house any more."

A lump rose in Lesley's throat as she remembered her high hopes of 12 months previously when Robert had retired. She'd imagined planning holidays, doing things on impulse and helping with the grandchildren. Apart from the grandchildren none of it had materialised.

In fact they were the ones who had started Rob's obsession.

"Granddad! We have to collect supermarket vouchers for a class computer," the eldest had declared when they collected him from school.

"And I need vouchers for sports equipment," the younger one had shouted, desperate not to be out done.

Robert had done both boys proud, doing half the weekly shopping in one supermarket and half in the other. To start with Lesley didn't mind the extra expense and the unfamiliar brands, plus all the items that weren't on the shopping list.

Then Robert had handed her a pile of plastic loyalty cards.

"Use these when you go shopping. We can save the points for holidays and treats."

Her soft leather purse had been ruined trying to squeeze in all the store cards.

But things got much worse.

"I'll just pop round to the corner shop for a pint of milk," Lesley had said, in the middle of making a rice pudding.

"No you won't. That shop doesn't reward loyalty.

I'll go to the supermarket."

It was another hour before the rice pudding could be put in the oven.

"It was worth the trip." Rob had been triumphant. "I got extra points for spending £5 on baby toiletries."

"We don't have a baby."

"I bought them just in case Jenny has another."

Lesley had suggested a short holiday by the sea to try and break his obsession.

"Not yet, when we've saved up enough points we'll use them to book a proper holiday."

She'd suggested a meal out at a fancy restaurant in town.

"No, let's go to that Italian franchise instead – I've got a 50% off voucher."

The kitchen drawers overflowed with tokens and cards and finally Lesley could take no more. It was ultimatum time.

Jenny parked in the field where the bustling car boot sale was well under way.

Lesley unzipped her suitcase and gleefully tipped Robert's treasure onto the stall. There were cheap bowls, mugs, baseball caps and a pile of CDs in cardboard sleeves; the rewards from a year of saving newspaper tokens.

Then she sat on a fold-up chair and willed her mobile to ring. Surely, Robert must have read the note by now and made his decision. Maybe the points meant more to him than she did. Lesley's hand trembled as their home number flashed up on the phone.

"Have you earned the one thousand Happy Marriage points required to make this call?" she asked her husband, trying to steady her voice.

"One hundred Happy Marriage points each for cutting up my five loyalty cards," he sounded nervous. "Two hundred points for destroying my teabag and cereal box tokens and three hundred for booking a table at Bon Appetit."

Lesley sighed in relief.

"Congratulations on achieving your target. Please come and collect your Happy Marriage reward – your wife."

OLD FRIENDS

"So, what are you doing nowadays, Caroline?"

The playgroup Christmas party falls silent like a television suddenly switched to mute. All eyes swivel towards my daughter and I struggle to breathe as the fear in her face wraps itself around my heart. Only the appearance of Father Christmas has had the same electrifying effect on this party before and he hasn't been invited for years.

This is the Playgroup Party in name only now. The toddlers still come but they are in their twenties and we mums are greyer, plumper and a little less harassed than when we organised the queue for Santa and handed out selection boxes. But the friendships made then have endured and each year we still hire the church hall and stick up paper chains and tinsel. We put on a buffet and catch up with the last 12 months' gossip.

"I'm down in London." Caroline answers David's

question shakily and I relax a little, hoping he won't ask her to explain further.

David's been in Hong Kong for the last two years - he's something big in banking - but his mum obviously hasn't kept him in the gossip loop about events at home.

"Don't be coy, Caroline," he persists. "I bet you're a top fashion designer or make over houses like on the TV. You were brilliant at art when we were at school."

Caroline had to screw up every last ounce of her courage to come here tonight but now she's fiddling with her hair like she did when something scared her as a little girl. My heart feels like it might break.

Somebody pushes a glass of mulled wine into my hand and whispers in my ear. "She's doing fine. She's holding her own against high-flying David Clarkson."

"I'm in media sales." Caroline manages a smile at her interrogator. "What about you?"

The others resume their conversations; Caroline has cleverly deflected any further questions or embarrassment. I grin at my daughter across the laden buffet table.

"Boring banking," he replies. "What do you sell? Something glamorous I bet. Give me your number - I work in London too."

This is going too far. Caroline is deathly pale and her eyes are searching for me. I almost knock the Christmas tree over in my haste to reach her. In the last two years Caroline has been to hell and back. This job has given her a new confidence that I haven't seen since needle marks started appearing on her arms and valuables started disappearing from the house. After our last terrible row she just vanished.

"Hello, David," I say, putting my arm around Caroline.

"Hi, Mum." There is false jollity in her voice. "David was just asking for my mobile number."

"Give him mine." I throw her a meaningful look. "You said you were changing yours."

Caroline doesn't have a mobile. A few weeks ago she called from a pay phone to tell us she was having treatment.

"Your address then," David presses.

"I don't…it's temporary. What I mean is…"

Caroline is flustered and raises her arm to brush the fringe from her eyes. Her loose-fitting sleeve falls and David sees the scars.

Suddenly I can't bear the secrecy anymore. The measure of success in life is different for everyone and on Caroline's own scale she has become the equivalent of a managing director.

"Caroline's on the way up," I tell David. "Her father and I are very proud that she's succeeding as a Big Issue seller and is building her own life. It's an honour that she's come home for Christmas."

Caroline looks at me aghast as I speak the unspeakable and David's mouth opens and closes before he regains his composure.

"Wow!" he says and then adds. "Do you have a dog?"

"Yes." Caroline almost smiles at the mention of her beloved Dotty. "I'm your stereotypical Big Issue seller."

"Having to leave my dog behind in Hong Kong broke my heart."

"We could maybe meet to walk mine in Hyde Park…"

"Fantastic. Call me when it's convenient." He hands her a business card.

David's eyes show that, unlike so many others, he does not pity my daughter.

GENIUS DECISION

The puff of green smoke made Barbara's eyes sting and she blinked hard for a few seconds. When she opened them the tiny genie was grinning at her.

"I have the power to grant you a single wish - I'm a probationer genie, you see, but I'm learning fast."

The small figure stood aggressively on top of the copper kettle, legs apart and hands on hips. Her eyes flashed with impatience and her voice was brusque.

"After entering you in my logbook I'll have enough genie hours to apply for promotion."

With a bright pink turban and elaborate gold trouser suit the genie looked like a miniature extra from Aladdin.

"So what's your wish? I haven't got all day to wait here whilst you weigh up the pros and cons between world peace and winning the jackpot on the lottery."

She sounded just like Barbara's mother had fifty years before, as she hurried her seven-year-old daughter to spend sixpence in the sweetshop; a shop that was lined from floor to ceiling with brightly filled jars and had a penny tray bursting with fruit salad chews, liquorice and white chocolate mice.

"Hurry up – I've your father's tea to cook. What about humbugs? Surely it can't be that difficult to make your mind up."

When she was put on the spot Barbara's mind always went blank. As a child, eager to appease her mum, she had grabbed the six nearest things from the penny tray and regretted it later when she found two blackjacks in her selection. She absolutely detested blackjacks.

As an adult her decisions never seemed right. The new dress that looked so good in the shop didn't suit her at home. The hotel with a sea view would have been better than the one she had booked with noisy nightly entertainment.

"Have you decided?" The genie was fiddling with an array of bejewelled bangles on her arm. "You've made a right mess of that duster."

Barbara was surprised to see that she had twisted the yellow faded fabric into a tight knot as her mind battled to think of a wish.

"My promotion to Three Wish Genie depends on me fulfilling my single wish tasks promptly and accurately. How can I do that if you can't decide what you want? I've been cooped up in that kettle for half a century so I'm already behind on my targets. Shame you didn't give the old thing a clean earlier."

Barbara felt like the little girl in the sweetshop again. Her brain was already befuddled with the decisions involved in arranging her mother's funeral, putting the house on the market and now clearing her mum's attic. It was difficult to decide what to discard, what to keep and what to sell.

"I'd just like a few minutes to decide, please. Would you like a cup of tea whilst you wait?"

"I'll have coffee with two sugars and a chocolate biscuit."

Barbara tried to gather her thoughts in the kitchen. Money was the obvious choice but her mother's house would fetch a tidy sum. Since Alec had died she'd been lonely but even genies couldn't bring husbands back from the dead and things were improving since she'd been cajoled into joining the Rambling Group. There she'd met Brian who'd invited her for coffee – she just had to decide whether to go or not.

"Wish for something you really want and make it snappy."

The genie was dancing with impatience behind her in the kitchen.

"I must get this right," muttered Barbara. "Oh, I wish I was good at making decisions."

"Wish granted."

"No! That wasn't my wish."

"Yes it was."

The genie disappeared in a puff of pink smoke along with a handful of biscuits.

Barbara was aghast at the wasted opportunity. Then her mobile burst into life and Brian's number flashed up.

"Just wondering whether you've given our coffee date any thought?"

"I'd love to come," said Barbara, without any hesitation.

By the end of the day the contents of the attic

were sorted into rubbish, charity shop and EBay piles and, when the estate agent rang with a low offer for the house, Barbara turned him down confidently.

That evening she went home feeling extremely satisfied with herself and the fresh outlook she had on life.

LIFTING THE CUP

As Robert entered the function room his eyes flew to the stage and rested on the red-clothed table that stood at its centre. The silver trophies displayed there had been polished like mirrors and looked resplendent in the sparkling light of the overhead chandelier.

It was the largest and most magnificent of the cups that interested Robert.

"I'm going to have a quick look," he whispered to his wife, Chloe.

"No, you are not," she hissed and grabbed his arm. "You are going to buy me a drink and not leave me standing alone with your beer-swilling mates. That trophy has dominated our lives all season – it's too late to change anything now so let's relax and enjoy the evening."

But Robert couldn't take his eyes off the massive Player of the Year award and his heart thumped every time he imagined how it would feel to lift it high on that stage and show it off at last.

"It's such a great honour to get it," he whispered to Chloe. "Imagine being able to boast that you were the very first winner of the James Whitman Player of the Year Trophy. Nobody who comes after you can ever beat that. Whoever gets it tonight will have their name engraved at the very top – future generations will always read their name first."

"You're obsessed," said Chloe. "If this were a televised awards ceremony for a Premiership Club I could understand it – but it's all amateurs."

"That trophy could lead on to greater things for me and my career," Robert pointed out. "There could be scouts from other clubs here tonight and if word gets around the amateur leagues then it'll only be time before the big boys get interested. A Wembley trophy might be next, and then the world will be my oyster."

Chloe shook her head and cast her eyes skywards, tiring of his endless trophy talk. "Do you see those pigs flying past?"

"I wish you'd be a little bit more supportive." Robert huffed, and stalked off to the trophy table.

The club's crest was the centrepiece of the two-foot-high cup. It sat on a mahogany base and their benefactor's name, James Whitman, appeared around the lip of the award, along with the dates that he had chaired the club. His premature death 12 months earlier had shocked everyone but his generous bequest had meant the club could install floodlighting as well as replace their worn and scratched Player of the Year Trophy.

"Ladies and gentlemen – please take your seats," a voice instructed.

The noise level in the room rose as last minute drinks orders were shouted across the bar and chairs were scraped as people got themselves comfortable. Robert made sure that he and Chloe didn't get sandwiched in by other people – he wanted to be able to glide gracefully from his seat to the stage.

Nerves made him twirl the platinum band on his left hand. He'd designed their wedding rings as a matching pair and noticed now that Chloe too was anxiously fiddling with her own ring.

The lesser awards were distributed first. A stream of youngsters, starting with ten-year-olds and finishing with lads in their mid-teens, received encouraging applause as they carried away small Perspex trophies as souvenirs of the season. The winner of the Golden Boot was no surprise – everyone knew that Wayne Jones had scored more goals than any other player in the club's history.

"And finally," announced the compere, "the one you've all been waiting for – the inaugural James Whitman Player of the Year Award."

A murmur ran around the room. One way or another, this award had been causing a stir all season. Whitman had stipulated that it should be designed and manufactured locally. He'd wanted it to be a unique trophy to symbolise the completely individual talents that each footballer had. So there'd been fierce competition amongst the local silversmiths as well as the players vying to win the title.

Robert squeezed Chloe's hand and then couldn't let it go. His excitement had been replaced by nerves knotting his stomach and gluing him to his chair. Ever since the new chairman had phoned him to say he was in the running, he'd hoped this moment would come. It was a chance to get his talent into the public arena and could lead on to bigger football clubs.

But now fear was getting the better of him. What if he couldn't get up?

Chloe pulled her hand free and gave him a gentle push.

"Go on – this is your moment."

The room fell silent as he walked up to the stage. The compere shook his hand warmly and gently propelled him towards the coveted prize, now the only award left on the table. The room was silent. Unable to resist it any longer, Robert ran his shaking fingers over the trophy's twin handles.

"Ladies and Gentlemen, to present this award we have its designer and manufacturer, Robert Stokes."

A round of applause filled the room.

"Before we invite the winner on to the stage, I'm going to ask Robert to give you a closer look at his masterpiece."

Robert raised the cup above his head and thought he would burst with pride as the Press flashbulbs went mad.

OUT OF CONTROL

"Stop! Stop!"

I pressed my right foot to the floor but the brake lights of the car in front were getting nearer and nearer with a terrible speed. Despite the pressure I was forcing through my leg, we were not slowing down. There was no room to swerve. The clash of metal upon metal was inevitable. Everything was out of my control.

Braced for the impact, I closed my eyes and waited for my life to flash before me. I wanted hazy pictures of me as a child or on my wedding day or at the birth of my daughter, Georgina, to calm my last conscious moments. But the memories that came were not the best.

There was Georgina, aged two, kicking and screaming as I tried to get her to bed.

"No sleep! Want play!"

"It's bedtime not playtime. Cuddle up with teddy

and we'll play in the morning."

"No! No! No!"

For a year we lived in this constant, shrieking, fighting tantrum.

"She's trying so hard to assert her independence," the Health Visitor had explained. "She'll calm down."

I felt the car shudder and then I was plunged into Georgina's first day at school.

"Hold my hand and we'll go into the playground together." I wanted to soothe her inevitable nerves.

"No, I'm a big girl now!"

There had been a tearing pain in my heart as she snatched her hand from mine and ran through the school gates without a backward glance. I watched in envy as other mothers consoled tearful offspring and cajoled them up to the classroom door.

Then she was handing me a letter about Brownie camp with eyes full of enthusiasm and excitement.

"We're canoeing and climbing and lighting camp fires!"

How would she come back in one piece without me supervising and checking her safety? Fires meant matches and matches meant burns.

"No," I said in a voice that was sharper than I intended.

But she got her way and for seven days I never went out of earshot of a phone. Every time it rang I jumped out of my skin. When she came home I had tried to smother her in a hug but she'd fought me off and proudly displayed an expertly bandaged knee and a small burn on her hand.

The noise of the car engine had changed now and I could hear the growing, urgent shout of sirens. But I saw no blue lights, only a 15-year-old Georgina marching off on her first Duke of Edinburgh expedition with a huge and heavy rucksack on her back. After a long day's walking there would be no hot bath and home-cooked meal just the tent she had carried and a pot noodle.

"Mum, will you stop wrapping me in cotton wool!" She'd exploded when I'd tried to talk her out of it.

The sirens reached a crescendo and I sensed the car was no longer moving. In the darkness behind my eyelids I imagined a scene of devastation from The Bill.

Down the years, and especially since Georgina's father left us, I'd tried so hard to be a good mother and whilst I knew my 'hands-on' involvement was at an end, I found it hard to accept. But I never dreamed that this would be our finale.

Suddenly there was a cacophony of noise. Screams filled my ears. There was pain in my hands.

"Mum, stop shouting and screaming."

I opened my eyes. We were stationary. There was a gap of two feet between us and the car in front. I caught sight of an ambulance disappearing up the road, en route to an emergency.

"I passed my test two months ago, Mum. I know how to stop the car at traffic lights." Georgina slipped the gear stick into first and got ready to pull away again. "You have to start trusting me with my own life and sometimes yours too. You can't be in charge of me for ever."

I looked at the deep red indentations in the palms of my hands caused by my nails as I clenched my fists in terror.

"You're right," I grinned ruefully. "And I must cut

my nails."

CHAMPAGNE GIRL

Mum and I sat on her settee and watched as TV cameras took the nation behind the scenes of the grand final of the Search for a Singer talent contest. Caught off guard, Adam stood pursing his lips as he had in the old days when pre-gig nerves kicked in.

'The old days' were the summer of 1981, when I was between A' levels and university. I spent each morning in a warehouse, bundling together ten Christmas cards to feed into a shrink-wrapping machine. Tinny speakers spouted Radio 1, with its summer road-shows, 'Bits and Pieces' competition and over sentimental 'Our Tune'. I dreamed of having a love-affair to write to Simon Bates about.

A friend's boyfriend got up a band and a group of us went to see them play. Adam Murray was their singer and guitarist. After the performance he scribbled my number on a beer-mat and asked me out.

I liked him immediately, with his long hair and gorgeous smile. He was three years older than me and was fighting parental pressure to find a 'proper job'.

"I want to give music a chance first," he told me, "not some pen-pushing graduate training scheme. I'm going to leave my mark on the world."

Adam took me to the band's gigs in their battered old van and I got used to starting the applause in half-empty rooms of disinterested punters.

But no man can live by lofty ambitions and sparsely attended gigs alone. Adam got a part-time job selling ice-cream from a van.

He served me his first '99 and I nibbled my flake in a way that I hoped made me look like the woman in the cornfield with the long hair.

Adam was generous and romantic. We went for a picnic with strawberries and wine. Alcohol was new to me so Adam drank most of it. He spent his ice-cream wages on a posh meal out for the two of us and then walked me home at midnight – four miles out of his way.

"I love you, Alison," Adam said one night, with his arms wrapped tightly around me.

We were in a crowded pub on 29th July. Charles and Diana had just tied the knot and the nation was rejoicing. Maybe he'd been affected by the romance in the air or maybe he really meant it.

Either way, his words set off fireworks in my heart.

"I love you, too." It was the first time I'd said those words to anyone.

Adam was a songwriter as well as a singer and guitarist. One day he presented me with a cassette tape of a song he'd written about me. Called

'Champagne Girl', it was a ballad about falling in love with a girl who fizzed with life, a girl about to leave home with the world at her feet, a girl he wanted to hold tight forever.

The song had a classical feel to it and was a departure from the usual pop stuff that he did with the band. It made me walk on air whenever I heard it. Who knew, one day it might even become a proper record and get to number one in the charts.

But, like all good things, summer romances come to an end. I got my A' level grades and went to university. Economic and parental pressure forced Adam to join a despised graduate training scheme and my song never did become a proper record. Adam and I lost touch with each other.

I became a primary school teacher and married a wonderful man. He died nine years ago, just after our daughter, Suzanne's tenth birthday. Since then it's been just the two of us, until Suzanne left home for college this year.

Then, a couple of months ago, Adam popped up on one of those TV talent shows! They're not normally my cup of tea but I've been watching him along with Mum every Saturday night as he's made it through heat after heat. My daughter was incredulous when I told her about Adam and me. She made me pick up the phone and vote for him!

One week the talent show cameras went into Adam's home and filmed him cooking a meal, ironing shirts and walking his dog. The next day the newspapers carried the headline, A Very Eligible Bachelor. My heart soared when I realised that he was single too and still lived in the area. But he'd probably forgotten about our summer romance all those years ago.

"Who would've thought that old boyfriend of yours would get to the final of Search for a Singer," my mother said, as she increased the volume on the television.

I sat with a cushion in front of my face. Even though I'd had no contact with him for over 30 years, I didn't want to see Adam fail. Peering round the edge of the cushion I watched as he moved towards a microphone on the huge stage and picked up a guitar. The eyes of the nation turned towards him and, as the gentle notes of 'Champagne Girl' filled the air, he sang directly into the camera. I felt as though he was staring right at me.

"I don't recognise this," Mum said. "I like to hear a song I know."

"Shush!"

When he finished singing there was a close-up shot of Adam. His lips moved without sound. I was almost sure that he mouthed the words 'For Alison'.

My heart flipped and then thudded uncontrollably. Suddenly I was 18 again and being swept off my feet. I kneeled in front of the TV, trying to be sure of what I'd just seen. But now Adam was walking off stage, he turned for a moment, waved at the audience and then I'm sure his lips formed my name again.

The show's presenter met him in the wings. "Well done, Adam. You could tell that you put your heart and soul into that song. The audience loved it! It's such a beautiful song. Is there a story behind those lyrics?"

Adam cleared his throat, looking shyly at his feet. Then he met the presenter's eyes.

"I wrote it for a very special girl, a long time ago.

A girl I've never forgotten. I guess you could say she was the love of my life."

Mum was looking from me to him.

"There was an article about Adam in here." Mum handed me the local paper. "Look, he's making a personal appearance at a music shop in town," she said.

I knew exactly what she was hinting at. And maybe she was right. Maybe it was time for us to catch up after all these years.

I wondered if he would recognise me if I went along…

MRS MUGGINS

"Are Robert and the children getting you something nice for your birthday?" Caroline's mother asked.

"Mum, it'll be the same as every year - bubble bath and chocolates." Caroline balanced the phone in the crook of her neck so that she could flip the bacon she was frying for tea.

"What's wrong with that?"

"Well," Caroline grumped, "I only ever take showers and if I so much as look at a single Ferrero Rocher, I put on a stone."

"I see."

"And Robert uses the same corny joke every year," Caroline continued her moan. "He says he's booked a meal for a beautiful woman but she can't make it - so he'll have to take his wife instead. I wouldn't mind but it's always that cheap Chinese place."

"Ask for what you want this year," her mum said. "Don't simmer with resentment because you've been taken for a mug again."

"Thanks for the tip," Caroline sighed. "I've got to go – this bacon's ready and I can hear Ben's stomach growling."

She tried dropping a hint to her son casually as she cleared his greasy plate. "Ben, the coffee beaker I use at work is horribly chipped - a new one for my birthday would be lovely."

He gave an indecipherable teenage grunt and disappeared into his darkened and slightly whiffy bedroom. Caroline knew it had gone in one ear and out the other. Her daughter would be a better bet.

"Helen, I could do with a new cup for the office. The cracks on mine must be full of germs."

"Whatever," muttered Helen, not looking up from her celebrity magazine.

Robert wasn't any more receptive even though she got straight to the point.

"I want a new bone china beaker for my birthday but the children aren't taking the hint. It's not much to ask for – may be you could get me one?"

"Where do they find these idiots?" Robert changed the channel from the latest reality TV auditions.

"I'm invisible to this family unless they're hungry or need clean clothes!" Caroline fumed.

"No you're not," Robert smiled. "I can see you perfectly well – you're blocking my view of the TV screen."

"And I hate that tacky Chinese place we always go to," she continued but Robert was lost in a rant at the referee.

The only mug around here is me, thought Caroline.

When she woke on her birthday she forced herself

into an appreciative mood. She was ready to smile gratefully at whatever bubbles or chocs came her way.

But this afternoon she would treat herself in town to a new coffee beaker and maybe a Mocha laced with cream, at the new café.

"Happy Birthday!" Ben dropped a parcel on the kitchen table.

Caroline eyed the messily wrapped package covered in sticky tape. It was suspiciously chocolate box shaped. With a sigh of resignation she ripped it open.

Diet chocolate. She'd had it before – it was sickly sweet and had no substance.

"See, I remembered you were on a diet and got the low calorie kind," Ben explained.

"That's lovely," Caroline said, hoping he didn't notice her gritted teeth.

Ben disappeared to football and Caroline took the cellophane off the box of chocolates. When disappointment hit, any chocolate was better than no chocolate. She ate the lot.

She was feeling slightly sick when Helen handed her a prettily wrapped package. Caroline knew this was the bubble bath - she could feel it was a bottle in a tall box.

"It's shower gel," Helen announced before the wrapping was fully off. "I noticed last year's bubble bath ended up in the charity shop."

Caroline started to grin with pleasure but it became forced as she read the label aloud. "With a long-lasting de-odorising effect - that'll be really useful, love, thank you."

Minutes later in the privacy of her bedroom Caroline sprayed herself liberally with Chanel. She didn't want anyone thinking she had a body odour problem.

Then Robert walked in.

"I didn't invite a beautiful woman to dinner this year," he said. "There's a special lunchtime offer on so I don't mind giving you first refusal."

Caroline swallowed the lump of disappointment in her throat, but it was too much this year. She felt a bubble of anger rising and, for once, let it all out.

"No one in this family listens to a word I say - you're all taking me for a mug," she fumed.

"It was going to be a surprise - how did you know?" Robert looked astonished. "Did the children let it slip?"

"How did I know what?" Caroline snapped.

"I'm taking you for a mug." He brandished a glossy brochure. "Pottery Place is doing a day package – design and paint a china mug, followed by lunch at that posh restaurant next door. We all thought you'd love it and Ben insisted we keep it a total secret. Then you started asking us all to buy you a china beaker. We tried to ignore you and the kids bought their usual presents so that we didn't ruin the surprise."

Caroline smiled. This was one mug she didn't mind being taken for.

NIGHT SHIFT

Robert rolled over to cuddle his wife.

"Not again!" he muttered when he found only an empty space and a dent in the pillow where Louise's head should have been.

He lay on his back and stared at the ceiling. What had happened to that lazy companionable retirement they had planned together? No sooner had he placed his brass carriage clock on the mantelpiece and collected a pile of cruise brochures from the travel agent's than his wife had announced that she had a new job.

It was a new job that not only filled her week but now occupied one weekend in four too, including these never-ending on-call nights. She might as well be back nursing at the hospital, like their grown-up daughter.

"The Boss was in a bad mood today," Louise regularly told him over their evening meal.

Robert knew what James could be like and had witnessed his angry reactions when events didn't go entirely his way.

At first this had upset Louise, even though she'd had several years' experience, but now, to her credit, she stood up to him.

"I'm sorry, James," he'd often hear her say as he passed the front room on his way to put the kettle on. "It's my tea-break now but I'll help you with that after my cuppa."

Most of Louise's work was home-based and so Robert often bumped into James, and he could understand how his wife had been won over by his contagious smile, brimming confidence and bagfuls of charisma. On a good day James could charm the birds from the trees but, on a bad one, he could drive you up the wall and during these night-time crises he was unbearable.

But Louise always accepted and excused these moods.

"James was a bit impatient today," she would say, after he'd left for the day. "But it was because he was under the weather."

Sometimes Louise was beaming when Robert got back from his round of golf.

"James helped me tidy everything up before he went home," she would explain.

Or, "Look! He gave me one of his paintings today."

Robert knew that James particularly enjoyed painting but the pictures he produced were too much like modern art for Robert's taste.

"That's great," he would say to humour Louise.

But for Robert the worst days were when Louise

was expected to chauffeur James to some function or other because that left Robert without a car.

He either had to beg a lift with a friend or squash his golf bag into the boot with James' paraphernalia and fit in with James' timetable for the day. Louise got petrol money but Robert didn't think it enough for the inconvenience to him of having no independent transport.

Robert could hear murmuring now from the adjacent bedroom. Louise was obviously trying not to disturb him whilst she dealt with whatever issue had caused tonight's call. Robert switched on the bedside light. Once he'd been woken sleep always eluded him until his wife was back in bed. He decided to make them both a cup of tea.

"Sorry, Robert," she called when she heard his feet on the stairs. "I'll be as quick as I can, but you know James; he's never satisfied."

The dog-eared cruise brochures stared at Robert from the kitchen table.

"I'm going to book this tomorrow," he resolved. "James or no James, we need a holiday. I'm sure someone else could take Louise's place for a couple of weeks."

He carried a tray back upstairs with two mugs of tea and a couple of chocolate biscuits. Louise was just climbing back into bed. She put a finger to her lips indicating he should be quiet.

"James would go mad for one of these in the middle of the night," she whispered waving a biscuit. "But he's not allowed them."

"About that cruise..." Robert's voice was barely audible; he wasn't going to risk a second crisis tonight. "I'm going to book it tomorrow regardless of

James' arrangements."

He was interrupted by a noise. Louise sighed and flung back the duvet.

"No, you stay there," said Robert. "I'll find out what the problem is first."

"Stay calm," pleaded Louise.

The dim night-light in the spare room was always left on when Louise was on call. Robert could just make out James. He was standing up facing the door, his mouth wide open ready to yell again. Robert pre-empted him.

"Now then, little man, why are you causing your grandma all this trouble?"

James' face broke into a wide grin.

"Granddad! Granddad!"

Robert lifted his grandson out of the cot and settled down to read The Hungry Caterpillar yet again.

"I think we'll leave that cruise until you're older," he said and ruffled James' hair. "Or until your mummy and daddy win the lottery and can give up their shift work at the hospital. Mind you, if that happened, your grandma and I would miss all these lovely cuddles."

CHRISTMAS LIGHTS

"She probably fancied a couple of extra hours in bed," said Derek. "It's snowy outside, and everyone's beginning to settle down for Christmas next week."

"But her curtains have never stayed closed this long." Linda exchanged slippers for shoes and reached for her coat. "She could've fallen down the stairs or got stuck in the bath."

"You're exaggerating. Besides, she only moved in three weeks ago and you've hardly exchanged two words with her." Derek put the kettle on for their elevenses. "I bet you don't even know her name."

"She's called Edna and I couldn't bear it if there was a repeat of the Mr Williams episode." Linda shuddered.

Mr Williams used to live in the same house that Edna now occupied and had been there for as long as anyone could remember. He always had a kind word for anyone who wandered past whilst he was mowing the lawn or watering his hanging baskets.

The children loved his limitless supply of humbugs and he willingly signed school sponsor forms and took on workers during Bob-a-Job Week.

But it was his Christmas lights that made Mr Williams the best known resident of the road. He started putting them up earlier and earlier each year. Last year Linda had watched him start at the beginning of November.

"My legs aren't what they were," he'd explained as he carried a cardboard box of multi-coloured bulbs from his garage. "I can only put up a few each day but I don't want to disappoint the kids. I know they look forward to the big December 1st switch-on."

Mr Williams didn't let anyone down with his final display. His house was illuminated on time and, as usual, his glorious festive lights made it feel like Christmas proper had begun.

There were pale blue icicles dangling from the gutters, flashing red and white balls around each window, an almost life-size Santa trying to climb down the chimney and a rainbow of sparkling stars dancing in his fir tree. Linda's favourite part of the display was the mother and baby reindeer nuzzling together in the centre of the lawn, for her it encapsulated the feeling that Christmas is for families.

The day after Twelfth Night, Mr Williams usually started dismantling cables, coiling strings of lights around his arms and generally returning his house to its ordinary state. But this last time it had been different.

"I wish he'd get those wretched lights down," Derek had moaned to Linda in the middle of January. "Some of us have been back at work a fortnight."

"He's not as young as he was." Linda excused their elderly neighbour. "The rain's probably kept him indoors."

"It's not like Mr Williams to leave the lights up so long," the man in the newsagents said, when Linda picked up her magazine. "And he's not been in for his paper the last few mornings either."

Linda began to worry. She wondered if Mr Williams would think her nosy if she knocked on his door to see why he hadn't removed his Santa and reindeers.

The next day the Neighbourhood Watch rep. gestured towards the un-lit decorations as he handed Linda the latest crime bulletin. "He'll get some bad luck with all his Christmas stuff still there."

"And those reindeer will get vandalised," observed Kathleen from the house opposite, as she joined them on the doorstep.

"Maybe we should see if he needs any help?" A twinge of guilt pulled at Linda's conscience. "After all, Mr Williams is getting on a bit."

"I've got no head for going up ladders," said Kathleen.

"Let's give it until next week," the Neighbourhood Watch man suggested.

As they left, Linda stared at Mr Williams' house again, willing a curtain to twitch or a light to go on against the descending tea-time darkness. Anything to stop this growing unease that something must be wrong. Linda had never set foot over Mr Williams' threshold and despite his usually friendly manner she didn't want to intrude into his private space.

The little fawn reached up towards his mother through the greyness of the January drizzle. Their

Christmas magic had gone, just as the spirit of goodwill had evaporated from the street.

Finally, Linda could stand it no longer. If she lived alone she would appreciate a friendly face at the door and hoped Mr Williams would feel the same.

There was no answer to her knock so she called through the letter-box. A faint moan answered from upstairs.

The ambulance came within minutes and he was stretchered off.

Two days later Mr Williams' son arrived with a giant bouquet.

"We're so grateful to you," he said, handing Linda the flowers and explaining his father would now be leaving the street and moving in with him. "It was pneumonia. You saved his life - you're a hero."

But Linda knew she had been a coward for not checking on her neighbour earlier.

Now, she pressed Edna's doorbell.

"How lovely to know you care!" the old lady said, when Linda explained why she'd come round. "I slept in after staying up much too late watching an old film. Will you have some coffee and a mince pie?"

COLLATERAL DAMAGE

"Alan, watch out!" Joan's words were almost a scream as her dinner party guest clumsily reached for the switch on the standard lamp.

But he moved his arm too quickly, dislodging the silk-fringed shade and causing the whole thing to wobble and fall.

It landed heavily against the polished teak dining table, smashing the bulb and plunging the room into semi-darkness. The falling lamp's vibrations made the gold candelabra on the table teeter and it cast eerie shadows along the walls as its lighted candles struggled to retain their balance. Finally this metal centrepiece toppled on to its side too, smashing against the uncorked red wine bottle, which in turn fell and hit a wine goblet.

It was like watching one domino hit another, as slowly the immaculate table setting was destroyed. There wasn't a sound in the room as the gravy jug hit the cream dining room carpet.

In the stillness that followed three pairs of eyes swivelled towards the trigger of this disaster.

"I'm really sorry - I just wondered how the standard lamp worked." Alan was shaking his head and wringing his hands. "Some of them have different switches. Shirley wants one so I was investigating."

His wife threw him a look of contempt. "Leave me out of this. I suggest you two men keep out of the way whilst Joan and I put this mess to rights. We don't want any more accidents."

Shaking slightly, Alan leaned over and put the gravy jug back on the table. He apologised again and then followed David, Joan's husband, into the lounge.

"Don't worry," Joan called after them in a voice that was much too shrill. "We'll have everything back to normal soon and then I'll serve dessert."

Tears were threatening at the back of Joan's eyes and she had a lump in her throat. The dining room was her pride and joy.

Even though the gold candelabra and wine goblet had never seen a carat, she enjoyed the way the gentle artificial candle-light embraced and enhanced their sheen.

The standard lamp gave the room a cosy glow that was much better than any stark overhead light. She hoped it was only the bulb that was broken and not the fitting it screwed into. At least the honey-coloured silk lampshade looked undamaged – she'd had an awful job trying to find a shade the right size that would also match the rest of the decor. None of it had come cheap.

"I can't apologise enough for Alan." Shirley was repeating herself in her embarrassment over her husband's faux pas. "He always has to touch things – you know what men are like and they're so clumsy. Of course, he'll pay for any damage."

"Don't worry," were the only words that Joan could manage and she had to concentrate so that a string of expletives didn't pour out as well. "Why don't you go and cut the chocolate gateau in the kitchen? It's easier for me to clear the dining-room up on my own. There's not really enough room for two of us."

Once she was alone Joan carefully examined the table for scratches. There was a small one where the standard lamp had hit but she could probably polish that out.

Then she completely cleared the dining table and used the dustpan and brush from the kitchen to safely sweep all the broken pieces of bulb. She'd bought the dustpan set to complete her kitchen equipment and hadn't expected to ever have to use it - but it did the job despite its size making it difficult to hold.

The wine bottle, goblet and gravy jug had all been empty so the carpet was unmarked. Joan carefully replaced them and everything else on the table.

"The gateau's ready to serve," said Shirley coming back into the room with the cake and a jug of cream on a tray. "Gosh, you've sorted that mess out quickly."

Shirley put the dessert down and called the men.

Joan could see the relief on Alan's face when he saw that the room had been put back to rights.

In place of the glow from the miniature standard lamp, now missing its bulb, she turned the full-size free-standing uplighter on and moved it nearer to the dolls' house so that Alan could better reassure himself that the miniature dining-room was OK. He moved to one side to get a better view, catching his foot in the flex of the uplighter.

"Alan, watch out!" Joan's words turned into a real scream as the heavy lamp toppled towards the fragile roof of the dolls' house.

BUILT TO LAST

Yvonne tapped her fingers irritably against the empty coffee cup. This was not the silver wedding anniversary she had hoped for - abandoned under a sunshade outside a Florentine café whilst her husband visited a hardware shop!

Bob was a DIY obsessive, but she'd hoped for a bit of culture and romance on their special weekend.

They still had the Uffizi gallery to visit and the Ponte Vecchio, with its scores of jewellery shops, and she didn't want to miss the world-famous statue of David.

Of course, she should have known better than to expect anything special on this holiday. When they were courting, Yvonne had watched each of her friends being treated to fancy restaurants and bouquets of flowers. All she got was a burger and a hug to keep her warm at the speedway track!

"I don't know how you put up with it!" her best friend Maureen had exclaimed, comparing her own giant, padded Valentine card and silver bracelet to the crash helmet Yvonne had received.

"We can spend more time together now that I can ride pillion." Yvonne had defended Bob despite her disappointment.

But even his marriage proposal had been based on practicalities.

"Mum's fed up of the motorbike in the hall," twenty-two-year-old Bob had explained. "She says it needs a permanent home. What do you think?"

"She's right. Your parents' house is tiny."

"Great!" Bob had beamed at Yvonne. "We'll ride it round Wales for our honeymoon, and I've seen an end-of-terrace with a large shed for sale."

Bob had just assumed that together they would find a better home for his motorbike.

This non-proposal had made it hard to suppress her envy when Maureen had talked endlessly about how her new fiancé had gone down on one knee and produced a surprise solitaire diamond from his jacket pocket.

And now, the same motorbike was still in the same shed. Bob kept it in pristine condition and only took it out for a run on summer Sundays.

"Sorry!" Bob reappeared at the café, panting slightly and clutching a brown paper bag. "It took longer than I thought. The man didn't speak English."

"What did you buy?"

"Just a few bits and pieces. I'm going to build some storage space in the loft when we get home. No more broken cardboard boxes, we need proper cupboards up there." He slurped his coffee, appearing not to notice its rather cool temperature.

"What's on next, madam tour guide?"

"Ponte Vecchio," Yvonne said, pulling out her guidebook and resisting the urge to hit her infuriating husband over the head with it. "It's the only bridge in the city to escape being blown up during WWII, and is famous for its goldsmiths' shops."

Bob, uncharacteristically, took her hand as they wandered down the narrow streets towards the bridge. It was a warm afternoon and there was a relaxed buzz in the air, as snatches of many different languages exclaimed over the beauty of the city.

Yvonne forgot to be annoyed with her husband and squeezed his hand with affection. He squeezed back, and she felt herself grinning.

Florence was every bit as wonderful as Maureen had described. Her friend had holidayed here to celebrate her first divorce.

"That shop had a good selection of screws, love." There was undisguised enthusiasm in Bob's voice. "I didn't get carried away, though - thought the X-ray machine at the airport wouldn't like it much!"

Yvonne's mouth lost its smile as disappointment seeped through her. She'd spent weeks researching this city - its art, churches and culture - but all Bob really cared about were a few nails he could have bought at home.

Maureen had been taken on some fantastic sight-seeing holidays by her second husband, George, and he'd researched them and organised them himself.

"Is this the bridge?" Bob suddenly seemed

interested.

They were swallowed up by the thickening crowd and swept on to the Ponte Vecchio.

"What's all that?" Yvonne pointed to a metal railing decorated with lots of shimmering padlocks and surrounded by young couples obviously in the first flush of love.

Yvonne thumbed desperately through her guidebook for an explanation. Maureen's George would have known what was going on, but Bob just stood there with a silly smirk on his face. It was a shame that Maureen and George had split up the previous year.

"There's nothing about this in here." She gave up flicking through the pages. "I'll have to try asking one of them."

Bob's smile broadened as he watched his wife approach one of the olive-skinned young men.

"Mi scusi…Perche…" Yvonne's night-school Italian failed her, and she gestured at the padlocks and tried to express a question mark with her face.

"Is… symbol of love," the young man explained, and put an arm round his girlfriend.

Yvonne thanked him and retreated, feeling slightly envious of those relaxed couples who weren't afraid of showing off their love for each other. They reminded her of the way Maureen and her new boyfriend, Jack, looked at each other.

Bob reserved such looks of adoration for his motorbike.

"Lucky I came prepared," Bob said, delving into his paper bag. He held out a large, coppery-coloured padlock and key. "This is a symbol of the long-term security of our love," he explained as he snapped the lock around the railing. "Now we throw the key into the river and the lock can never be opened. Nothing will come between us, sweetheart. Our marriage will last for ever."

As he saw Yvonne's confused expression change to one of delight, Bob said a silent thank you to the helpful man in the hardware shop. He wanted his wife to know how much he treasured her, but the right words always seemed to escape him.

There were tears in Yvonne's eyes as she hugged her husband.

"That was a lovely thing to do," she said.

And as they walked away, hand in hand, through the throng of happy couples, Yvonne realised that Bob was right. He might not be the most romantic man she knew, and she might have had to compete with a motorbike for his attention, but he loved her, and that was never going to change.

There was a lot to be said for that.

House Guests

SALLY JENKINS

CONTENTS

THE VERDICT

It was hot and airless in the jury room. The radiator belted out heat despite the sunny weather outside.

Keith loosened his shirt collar and tried to concentrate on the arguments ping-ponging between his fellow jurors.

"Both the eye-witness and the victim put the accused at the scene," said a well-spoken woman who had introduced herself as a retired school teacher. "The witness was sure it was him because his coat was so distinctive."

"They sell those purple parkas on the market," said a scrawny young woman wearing black eye-liner. "Anyone can buy them."

Keith knew the stall that sold the coats but kept his mouth shut. If they disregarded the eye-witness because the coat wasn't so unusual, there'd be more risky debate amongst the jurors and they might not reach a guilty verdict. It would all hinge on the circumstantial evidence, which could be argued either way, plus the victim's identification of the perpetrator.

So Keith said nothing and walked over to the window. He fiddled with the catch and finally let a slight breeze into the stuffy room. Then he turned to face his eleven colleagues. It was time to get them on his side and the decision made.

"OK. Let's go through it all again from the beginning."

Keith had had to fight to get himself elected as foreman of the jury. But, as he'd hoped, victory had given him an air of authority and it was something he could work to his advantage with the weaker jurors.

"It's almost 10pm on a Saturday evening and dark when the perpetrator enters the off-licence." Keith spoke slowly and made eye-contact with his audience, as though he were the star barrister in a TV courtroom drama.

"He is wearing a purple parka with the hood up and a black stocking pulled over his face. He has gloves on. The shop is empty; all the staff have gone home except for the manager who is cashing up. The CCTV doesn't work."

Eleven faces nodded in agreement at the basic facts.

"The accused pulls two carrier bags from his pocket and demands that the manager fill them with cash. And at that exact moment our middle-aged female eye-witness comes in."

That scene in the small shop was etched in Keith's mind. It had been described and re-described by the off-licence manager, the eye-witness and both barristers. He knew every detail.

"The manager refuses to part with the money,"

Keith continued.

"And the accused becomes violent," interrupted the retired school teacher. "He planned to hurt that poor man whether the money got handed over or not."

Keith's hackles shot up. This la-di-da woman was making incorrect assumptions without knowing all the facts. "The violence wasn't pre-meditated."

"How do you know?" asked the girl with the eyeliner. "We didn't cover that in the evidence."

"I … It's obvious - the accused didn't arrive at the off-licence armed. He picked up that wine bottle on the spur of the moment. If it was premeditated he would've taken a weapon."

"But he knew there'd be plenty of bottles in the shop," said the school teacher triumphantly. "There was no need for a gun or a knife."

The others were nodding in agreement.

Keith felt like the jury was turning on him. He went to the window and took a few deep breaths of fresh air. He must keep his temper. When Keith wasn't in control of a situation he became angry. That mustn't happen today or he'd end up in the dock of this very court.

It didn't matter what the jury thought about the violent tendencies of the man in the dock. This wasn't anything personal against Keith. In fact the worse they thought of the accused, the more likely a guilty verdict.

"Sorry. I've taken us off at a tangent," Keith said. "It's not important whether or not the violence was pre-meditated. All we have to decide is whether that man in the dock is the same man who knocked the off-licence manager unconscious with the wine bottle and then scarpered with the weekend takings."

"How can we do that without DNA or fingerprint evidence?" whined a middle-aged man with wire-rimmed glasses.

Keith thought he looked like a wannabe scientist who hadn't quite made the grade.

"The verdict only has to be 'beyond reasonable doubt'. We don't have to know it with 100% certainty," said the school teacher.

"I couldn't live with myself if we sent the wrong man down." The wannabe scientist pulled out a grubby handkerchief and dabbed at his brow which was glistening with sweat.

The teacher poured some water into a paper cup and passed it to him.

They argued for another two hours. Despite the cool breeze Keith's shirt was sticking to him and he was beginning to feel sick with nerves. The verdict was swinging one way and then the other. To Keith it was cut and dried, the witnesses had identified the accused so therefore he was guilty. But not all the jurors thought that way.

"You can't properly recognise someone with a black stocking over their head," said the girl with the eyeliner.

"And he swears he didn't do it," the wannabe scientist added.

"But they all plead not guilty," said Keith. "Wouldn't you?"

Eventually Keith pushed for a vote and thankfully it was unanimous. They were ready to go back into the courtroom.

In the jury box Keith stood up to give the verdict. He paused before announcing their decision.

He looked around the courtroom. There was absolute silence. All eyes were on him and he felt powerful.

The off-licence manager was staring at him from across the court. Until now the man had appeared only to give his evidence. He had been absent for the rest of the proceedings. In the witness box the manager had been nervous, stumbling over the oath, focussing his gaze on the ceiling or the floor and completely ignoring the rest of the courtroom he was supposed to be addressing. This was the first time he'd even glanced at the jury.

For a second Keith and the off-licence manager locked eyes.

Keith was catapulted back into that dingy corner shop. The manager refused to hand over the cash. What choice had Keith had? The bottle hadn't even smashed but the man had crumpled unconscious to the floor. The eye-witness had run out into the street screaming. Keith had shoved the money into his bags and found a back way out into a deserted alley.

"It was him!" The off-licence manager was on his feet and gesticulating at Keith. "He's the one that attacked me."

There was confusion amongst the legal teams and the judge was leaning forward to whisper to the clerk of the court.

"Guilty!" shouted Keith in an attempt to direct the court's attention back to the accused man in the dock. "The jury finds the defendant guilty."

Being selected for this particular jury had been a golden opportunity for Keith to put someone else away for his own crime. Now it had all gone horribly wrong.

The judged nodded at a police officer and the

uniformed man walked towards Keith with a pair of handcuffs.

BOXES IN THE LOFT

Robert Sullivan was late.

When a battered Volvo finally pulled up outside, I opened the front door before its driver had even walked up the path.

"Robert Sullivan." He introduced himself. "I've come about the internet advert."

"Lisa Jones." I shook his hand.

He was unexpectedly tall, dark and handsome.

Then I noticed the ring on his left hand - like so many fanciable men, he was already taken. Don't even consider him, I told myself.

"Shall I fetch my stuff in?" he asked.

"Err… yes. I haven't done this before."

"Me neither." His smile was disarming. "We'll learn together, shall we?"

Robert Sullivan carried ten large cardboard boxes through my hall, up the stairs and to the foot of the loft ladder.

"Do you need some help?" I asked.

"No. I'm fine."

Robert was wearing a close-fitting T-shirt and black jeans. As he laboured up into the loft under the weight of each box I admired the stretch and flex of his well-defined upper-body muscles.

"£2.00 per box, per month - according to your ad on RentStorage.com." Robert produced a £20 note. He hesitated before continuing. "Is it alright if I bring some more next week, Lisa?"

I nodded.

To my delight Robert Sullivan began coming every week, bringing a couple more boxes each time. I kidded myself it was only his rent money I was interested in but I couldn't help straightening my hair and getting changed before he was due.

"Where's all this stuff coming from?" I asked one day.

"We're having a clear out."

"Doesn't that mean throwing things away - not storing them elsewhere?"

"I'm a hoarder but my wife hates clutter. She insisted I take all this to a charity shop."

"So storing it here is a secret compromise?"

He nodded.

As time went on he only brought one box each visit and carried it up the ladder in double quick time.

Then one week he turned up without his wedding ring.

"Is everything OK?" I asked, staring at his left hand as we drank coffee.

"Sort of. Months ago I discovered my wife was seeing a work colleague. She refused to finish it - even though I did everything to please her, like this decluttering."

My heart leapt at the thought of Robert's marriage ending. Then I scolded myself for being pleased at someone else's misfortune.

"And then I met ... someone else," Robert continued.

"Oh." I felt worse than when I thought he was happily married.

"I've only one more box to bring," he continued more cheerfully. "See you next week?"

After he'd gone I wondered how someone else had succeeded in winning Robert over when I'd failed, despite seeing him every week. Was there a secret way to his heart? At least his boxes in the loft meant we wouldn't lose touch completely.

The boxes! They might hold a clue to what made him tick. Nervously, I climbed the loft ladder. One of the boxes blocked my path from the ladder onto the loft boards. I leant against it to push it away but there was no resistance and I almost went flying as the box shot under the eaves.

I stood up and approached the cardboard cube cautiously. Why was it so light? Feeling like a criminal I eased the masking tape off the upper flaps and looked inside.

Empty! This box and the next and the next were all totally empty. Only the ten original boxes were loaded up with books and CDs. Why?

On Saturday Robert arrived at the usual time but he was wearing a shirt and tie. He looked so attractive it hurt. This 'someone else' was a very lucky woman.

"Last box." He handed me a shoe box inscribed 'For Lisa'.

Startled, I removed the lid to reveal a red rose and

a card.

"To my 'someone else'. Please come to dinner with me tonight," I read aloud. My heart thumped and I felt wobbly.

Later we gazed at each other over a candle-lit restaurant table.

"Why did you put empty boxes in my loft?" I asked.

"I needed a reason to keep coming round until I found the courage to ask you out."

HARD LABOUR

"Push again!" Steve urged.

"I can't," Jessie panted.

Her whole body was exhausted but she had to continue - there was no other option. She breathed deeply and prepared to work her muscles again. This was just the start of becoming a mum. She hoped it wasn't always going to be this physically demanding.

She heaved, groaned and pushed until she could take no more. "I can't do it!"

"Yes you can, Jessie," Steve encouraged. "Imagine the end product – think of our son. I guarantee all this pain will be worthwhile."

Our son - despite the hellish discomfort she was experiencing, her heart did a joyful loop-the-loop at those words. A family of their own was something that Jessie had thought might never happen. She and Steve had almost given up hope of becoming parents. They'd married late and then discovered their age was against them in all sorts of ways.

"Jessie, surprising things happen to all of us," her mother had said. "Never give up hope that one day you two will have a little one to love and nurture."

Steve and Jessie were both well past 40 and hope seemed like the only thing they had on their side. Time was passing them by with the speed of a bullet train.

Jessie had started watching those programs on the TV where couples travel half-way around the world to adopt a baby from an over-stretched orphanage. How she'd wished they had the money to fund a trip like that and rescue a child from a life of poverty.

Sometimes she thought that Steve was more despondent about their childlessness than she was. He was a midwife and had always said how special it would be for him to deliver their baby.

"You won't have to be in a room full of strangers, Jessie. It'll be me, you and the baby. We'll be a family straight away."

"It might never happen," she'd told him, wishing that they'd met each other earlier in life.

He said it didn't matter but she knew it did matter - to both of them.

When Steve discovered they were having a boy he was overjoyed.

"Our Jason will be United's number one fan. I'll get him a season ticket and all the kit and I'll buy some goal posts for the garden so that we can have a kick around. He might even get into the youth team!"

"Jason might hate football." Jessie had tried to curb her husband's soccer enthusiasm a little. "He might be a more artistic soul who likes painting or music. We have to give him a range of experiences.

Remember what they said at that parenting class."

"That'll be fine by me." The look of disappointment on Steve's face had only lasted a second and Jessie knew that he'd back young Jason all the way in whatever he wanted to do. After all the palaver they'd been through to have this child; Steve wasn't going to quibble about what the little one's hobbies turned out to be.

Jessie was breathing heavily now and her back was agony. Steve seemed to sense that she couldn't take much more.

"Hang in there," he called. "We're past the point of no return. Push again when you're ready. Soon the head will be visible to me and I'll be able to help from this end."

As Jessie felt her muscles preparing for yet another heave, she prayed that this time Steve hadn't bitten off more than he could chew. She really didn't have the strength to carry on much longer. Steve thought that they could manage this by themselves but he wasn't struggling to push like Jessie was.

"Isn't it time we phoned for help?" she pleaded. "John next-door did offer to come round if we got in a tight spot. It would really help to have someone next to me."

"It'll be fine. We're nearly there."

Jessie remembered how he'd said the same thing when fitting their new shower – they'd ended up with a flooded bathroom and no electricity. He'd also sworn everything would be fine when he changed the oil in the car but it had spewed the thick black liquid all over the drive. Steve was the sort of a man who refused to stop and ask for directions, even when hopelessly lost in the car.

But, as promised, everything had been fine when next-door's dog was in labour. Steve had calmed both the spaniel and her owner and all the puppies had been delivered safely.

Steve was an excellent midwife, regardless of whether his patients were human or animal, even if his DIY skills weren't up to scratch. But none of it meant that they were going to get safely through this.

"I'm going to push again," Jessie shouted as her muscles started to contract.

"Great. I'm going to try and get a grip so that I can pull from this end."

Jessie hoped she could push long and hard enough for him to help her. She also wished that he could experience just a little of the pain she was going through. Her muscles weren't built for this - this was a man's job.

As she braced herself again the kitchen radio started playing 'Lady in Red' by Chris de Burgh.

"It's our song!" she screamed as her muscles let rip.

The song was a reminder of their first meeting at a mutual friend's wedding when Jessie had worn a crimson bridesmaid's dress. It was the most beautiful gown she'd ever owned - the fashion pages would probably describe it as a sheath dress and it was extremely suitable for a mature but slim bridesmaid.

'Lady in Red' was the song chosen by the bride and groom for their first dance. Once they'd been around the dance floor a couple of times, Steve had come over and asked Jessie to dance. They'd moved slowly to the music, cheek to cheek, and since that night they'd never looked back and the song had always been special.

Suddenly, mid-heave, there was a release of pressure and Jessie almost toppled over when her muscles found nothing left to push against.

"I've pulled the head free! You did it! We did it!" Steve sounded like an over-excited child.

Jessie heard a faint cry above the noise of the radio and then realised it was her own cry of relief that the torment was over. She grabbed hold of the bannister to steady herself.

Worn out, she closed her eyes and pictured the expression on Jason's face when he saw the brand new Thomas the Tank Engine bed that they'd just manoeuvred up the stairs. The bed head had caused all the problems. It was oversized and in the shape of the train.

Jason was three-years-old and devoted to the blue engine with the smiling face.

From her position just below that awkward bend in the staircase Jessie could hear Steve dragging the wooden bed frame across the landing and into the newly decorated bedroom. It would all be set up perfectly by the time their newly adopted son, Jason, arrived from his foster home. He'd be here in just a few hours.

CHARITY CHALLENGE

Doreen pressed the 'Play' button on the answering machine as she came in from the night shift.

"Hi, Mum!" Katie's familiar voice filled the tiny lounge. "We've reached Derby. There's no hot water at the camp site and it's a bit primitive. I'll call again tomorrow."

Poor Katie – all hot and sweaty after a day in the saddle and she didn't even have the luxury of a warm shower to ease her aches and pains. Thank goodness her daughter wasn't one of these teenagers who carted a whole beauty counter around in her handbag. Doreen didn't imagine there'd be anywhere for primping and preening in the tent. But Katie would be fine - she could apply the little make-up that she did wear with her eyes closed.

"We're somewhere south of the Midlands," Katie announced on the machine the following day. "We did 70 miles today and the water is very hot!"

Doreen smiled to herself as she got ready for a good day's sleep after her shift at the hospital. It was typical of Katie to have no idea geographically where she was. As a small child it had taken her ages to get the hang of right and left, she'd never been able to read a map and the signposts en route would have passed her by unnoticed. Right now her daughter wouldn't want to exhaust the goodwill of the others in the group with too many questions about where they were.

"Twenty miles past Oxford, Mum and all is well!" announced Katie when Doreen pressed 'Play' early the next morning.

Joseph, the Labrador, gave a whine at the sound of his mistress' voice.

"Poor Joe - you're missing her as much as me, aren't you? But you're one of the reasons that she went on this mad expedition in the first place."

She gave the dog a cuddle and wondered where her daughter got her adventurous spirit from. Cycling from Leeds to Paris with a group of university students did not appeal to Doreen and certainly not when it involved camping every night.

"We're sitting in a pub in Portsmouth waiting for the 11pm ferry," proclaimed Katie's message the following day.

Doreen glanced at her watch. Katie had left the message 8 hours ago so they must be in France by now, maybe breakfasting in a little café on croissants and good coffee.

Doreen switched on the computer and emailed the local paper with an update on her daughter's progress. They'd done a feature on Katie before she left and it had brought in lots of offers of support. Katie had easily exceeded the £250 minimum sponsorship that each student had been asked to raise.

"Nous sommes en Lyons-la-Foret." Katie spoke in an exaggerated French accent next time Doreen pressed 'Play'. "Last stop before Paris and the luxury of a youth hostel bed!"

Doreen smiled at her enthusiasm. Katie wouldn't let anything stand in her away. In recent years there'd been a constant stream of technological advances that had enabled her to study independently and gain a place at university. But this bike ride was a challenge that no shiny, state-of-the-art laptop could help with.

The following day was Doreen's day off and she grabbed the phone as soon as it rang.

"Mum! I've just cycled round the Arc de Triomphe!" Her daughter was shouting over the background noise of traffic.

"Brilliant!" Tears rolled down Doreen's cheeks – her daughter had achieved something that she'd never thought possible.

"I'll be home on the Eurostar tomorrow and then we can start collecting the sponsorship money. Guide Dogs for the Blind will be astounded when they see the amount I've raised."

Joseph was sitting at Doreen's feet looking hopeful.

"You'll be back in harness tomorrow," Doreen reassured him, "when we collect Katie from the station."

Then she called the local paper. They had promised a follow-up interview with Katie about how she'd dealt with the challenges of the expedition, not just the physical strain of pedalling 70 miles a day but also the alien environments of a new campsite each night and the constant need to trust other people with her life.

The feature on the local girl, blind since birth, who had cycled to Paris on a tandem would make great copy.

GROWING OUT OF BURGERS

Winner of the Friends of Morley Literature Festival Short Story Competition 2013

Madame Dupont whipped the egg and then poured the sunshine yellow liquid into a dish of raw minced beef. Lindsay watched as she bound the meat and egg together with the fork. The only noise was the occasional scrape of metal on glass.

He'd just got up and the house was empty apart from him and his hostess.

She caught his eye and gave him a knowing smile. It was 10 am but she was still in her dressing-gown, not a huge fluffy candlewick thing like his mother wore but a thin, silky, red affair that was held together by a tie-belt. The gown was low-cut and Lindsay could see the flesh at the top of her bosoms. He knew he shouldn't look but that slight wobble of olive skin drew his eyes like a magnet. She must be naked under that dressing-gown and Lindsay had never seen a naked woman.

This school exchange visit was turning out better than he'd expected, given the bad start of the evening before.

French families had already claimed all his classmates. He'd been the only one left in the Lycee assembly hall.

"Lindsay Wilson?" the teacher had called at last.

"That's me." He stood up.

The teacher looked flummoxed. "You are a boy." She stated the obvious in heavily accented English. "I expected a girl."

"Lindsay can be a boy's or a girl's name." How many times in his 15 years had he given this explanation? Exactly the same number of times he'd cursed his parents for landing him with such a puffy name.

"But we have partnered you with a girl, Corinne Dupont, for the exchange holiday. This is not good."

A girl and a woman stood up on the far side of the hall.

"There is nowhere else for you to go," the teacher continued.

There was a hurried conversation between the teacher, the woman and the girl. Every few seconds the woman glanced sideways at Lindsay, as though she were inspecting him. Then she came and kissed him on each cheek.

"Bienvenue, Lindsay. I will like to have a man in the house. I will like to satisfy his appetite." She put an odd emphasis on this last word whilst looking him directly in the eye. "I am a good cook."

Lindsay felt his cheeks flush under her gaze.

She had to be Corinne's mother. But her face was unlike that of any mother he knew. There were no comfortable lines around the eyes or flashes of grey in her roots. This French mother had smooth olive skin, cropped black hair and her close fitting dress clung to a figure that was best described to others using cupped male hand movements.

"Salut!" Corinne had stepped forward to welcome him too.

She was smaller, thinner and less sexy than her mother – but better than a lot of the girls in Lindsay's year at school. For a start she had no spots.

"Did you sleep well?"

The question jolted him back to the present. He lifted his eyes from Madame Dupont's flash of breast, which was wobbling with the exertion of working the fork in the meat.

"Yes, thank you."

It was a lie but what else could he say? When he'd arrived at the house the previous evening Madame Dupont had produced a bottle of fizzy wine, damp with condensation. The house had echoed to a gun-shot as she opened it.

"Let us celebrate a man in the house!" she said, handing Corinne a small glass.

Then she poured liberally into Lindsay's. The liquid frothed over and ran on to the table.

"We will be good together, n'est ce pas?" she said and clinked her flute to his. "A man in the house is good."

He raised the wet glass to his lips and sipped. The sour bubbles hit his nostrils and made him cough. Madame Dupont had already finished her wine. Lindsay felt obliged to follow suit and discovered that the quicker he drank, the more bearable it was. By the third glass he was high on the fizz as well as the way Madame Dupont was treating him as a valued adult male.

"Sleep," she announced, suddenly.

Lindsay tottered as he stood up and was surprised to find that the floor was no longer level. Then Madame Dupont's arm was around him. His nostrils were filled with her spicy perfume combined with a more earthy smell which he identified as female sweat. Surprisingly, it was exciting instead of revolting.

At the top of the stairs he glimpsed Corinne's large bedroom with two twin beds, both made up. Obviously the female Lindsay Wilson had been supposed to share a room with her exchange partner.

"We have another room," Madame Dupont said quickly, stopping Lindsay from following Corinne into her pink and white boudoir.

The other room was more like a broom cupboard. There was a fold-up camp bed leaning against the wall and Madame Dupont indicated that he should set it up. He was still struggling with the metal frame when she came back with a sleeping bag and pillow. She stood close to him and helped his fumbling hands to loosen the catch. He felt the heat of her body and the pressure of her limbs through his clothes.

Then she kissed him goodnight on the cheek. He tried to return the compliment but she had gone.

Afterwards he'd lain awake for ages, entertained by tantalising thoughts of his hostess. He'd tried to push her from his mind but his teenage hormones and wine befuddled brain hadn't let him.

Now he had a headache.

"You look tired," she said, taking the tall wooden pepper mill and twisting.

A shower of black dots floated into the pink meat. Her flesh wobbled again as she pressed the flavouring through the mixture. Lindsay fingered the mobile in his pocket and wondered if he could get a photo.

"You were still asleep when Corinne went to school. I thought it more important that you rested than had lessons."

"Merci." Lindsay was glad he hadn't been wakened – his dreams about a continental woman with short dark hair had been much better than a school desk.

Madame Dupont sat down opposite him and placed a forkful of the beef in her mouth. Lindsay's stomach turned. He'd thought she was preparing homemade burgers for lunch. Wouldn't she catch Mad Cow Disease or Foot and Mouth? Then there was the raw egg – his mother was always going on about salmonella.

The French woman was chewing slowly, obviously enjoying what was in her mouth. The smell of raw flesh wasn't mixing well with Lindsay's headache.

"Et tu?" she asked and offered him a forkful of the mixture.

At home with his own mother, he would have made throwing-up noises to show his revulsion at the food. Instead, he opened his mouth and she placed the fork into it.

His body tingled at the intimacy of sharing. It felt like they were lovers. At the same time he was fighting not to gag on the raw meat as he chewed it and prepared to swallow. It was the consistency rather than the peppery taste that disagreed with him.

"More?" She refilled the fork and was offering it

again.

He opened his lips and she slipped it in, smiling.

"You are a proper man," she said. "My husband must have it cooked. But you do not fear disease."

Lindsay sat up taller at her words and tried to appear more macho than the gangly youth that he was. He swallowed the uncooked flesh quickly.

"Where is Monsieur Dupont?" He tried to keep his voice casual.

"In Dubai. I am alone for now." She uttered the last sentence with a breathy sigh.

With a shake of his head he refused a third mouthful, fearing he might throw up in front of this sex pot.

Madame Dupont finished the raw meat. He watched the movement of her lips and listened to the slight chewing noises that emanated from them. He looked at her slender neck as she swallowed. His eyes were drawn further down to the red 'V' of her dressing-gown.

"Pardon," she said. "I forget your breakfast. Tu as faim?"

"Oui, un peu." Lindsay hoped his French accent wasn't too clumsy.

She rose from the table and busied herself at the other end of the kitchen. Her red silk dressing-gown finished at the knee. The girls at school hid their legs under tights or trousers for most of the year. When they unveiled them in the summer, they were either pasty white or almost orange from too much fake tan. Madame Dupont's calves reflected the same olive smoothness of her face. Lindsay leant over the table to see her feet. She was wearing gold flip-flops and there was scarlet polish on her toe nails.

The smell of coffee began to fill the kitchen. This never happened at home. His mother opened the jar of instant, plonked a spoonful in a mug and scalded it with boiling water. Madame Dupont was making proper coffee. The aroma was intoxicating.

Lindsay felt like he'd stepped outside his real world of GCSEs and adolescent angst into a film set for a romance. Here he was, the handsome macho hero with a sexy woman willingly making breakfast for him. His whole nervous system was on red alert with the intensity of it. The slight undulations in the wooden surface of the kitchen table registered like mountains beneath his finger-tips. The slicing of bread sounded like the swipe of a guillotine blade. His head was swimming in the smell of coffee whilst the tang of blood was still fresh on his tongue. But best of all was the sight of the red-sheathed woman with her back to him. Beneath the thin material was a female, an attractive, older, experienced female, who was definitely interested in him. He wondered if the belt tied loosely around her waist might accidentally come undone.

"Coffee," she said and placed two bowls of milky brown liquid on the table. "And bread."

A bowl wasn't what he was expecting. He looked to Madame Dupont for a lead as to what to do with it.

"You can dip the bread."

Lindsay took a slice, buttered it and then dunked into the dish. A film of melted butter transferred to the surface of the coffee. He lifted the bread to his mouth and bit off the soggy light brown end. It felt like grown-up comfort food.

Madame Dupont was drinking from her bowl

now. Lindsay followed suit. As he placed it back on the table he felt dribbles of the warm liquid run down his chin. He put out his tongue to catch them. Then Madame Dupont leaned over the table and dabbed at his face with a cloth napkin. He could smell her coffee-scented breath. She licked her own lips as she dabbed at his. Lindsay's mother had cleaned his face a thousand times but Madame Dupont made it an intimate, sensuous gesture instead of a brisk display of motherly concern.

Between them they finished the bread and drained their coffee bowls. He looked at the kitchen clock. The hands had sped round and it was nearly lunchtime. He wondered if his hostess would get dressed. The belt had slipped slightly and a little more of her olive skinned bosom was on display.

"Shall we go upstairs?" she asked.

Lindsay's heart thumped wildly and he felt as though he might fall over if he stood up and tried to walk.

"Soon Corinne will be home," she said and offered her hand.

Lindsay swallowed hard, took her hand and followed her upstairs.

Before he left home his uncle had warned him about frogs' legs and snails, his granddad had said something about a nation of garlic-eating onion sellers pedalling around the country and his mother had gone into a panic about how many pairs of underpants and socks he might need. But nobody had warned him that he would be presented with the opportunity to lose his virginity to the mother of his exchange partner.

This sexual initiation was a moment he'd craved

but now that it was upon him he was beset with fears. How would he know what to do? What if he couldn't perform? Would she expect him to provide condoms – that was the one thing that his mother had not included in his suitcase.

They paused outside his box room and Madame Dupont pushed the door open for him.

"You will want to get ready," she said.

What was that supposed to mean? He could spray on a bit more deodorant and clean his teeth but was there something else he should do – some secret ritual they'd omitted from those embarrassing lessons at school about human reproduction?

"Shall I have a shower?" he asked, trying to discreetly sniff his armpits.

Madame Dupont looked puzzled. "If you wish but she will be here in thirty minutes."

Speed was obviously of the essence. Trembling Lindsay moved closer to his hostess. He embraced her, allowing his hand to linger over the silk-covered mound of her breast.

"Non!" She jumped away from him. "Non! Do not touch."

Madame Dupont tried to cover herself more fully with the red gown as she backed down the landing.

Lindsay was still shaking but now it was with confusion and humiliation. Somehow he had totally misinterpreted her signals. What did she think of him? Would she tell the school? Would he be branded a sex offender and be hounded by press and public for the rest of his life?

"Corinne is a half-day at school." Madame Dupont was almost in her own bedroom now and speaking very quickly. Her English had suddenly deteriorated.

"You go with her friends. I dress and do shopping."

Then she disappeared, firmly closing her bedroom door.

That French woman spoke a different language in more ways than one. Lindsay wished to be magically transported home so that he could pretend nothing had ever happened. But already there were noises downstairs. Corinne had arrived back with her mates. He took a deep breath and hoped he didn't look as bad as he felt.

Half an hour later he was staring at a bland-looking burger and a cardboard container of fries. Everything was identical to his usual fast-food hangout back in England but now it seemed like nursery fare. Too much had happened in the space of that short morning and such immature food would never satisfy him again.

But he ate well – he didn't want to face his hostess over the dinner table that evening.

FATHERS' CLUB

It was 8am and I was bleary-eyed from yet another sleepless night.

"Andrew! How's baby Ben?"

I stopped dragging the wheely bin towards the end of the drive and turned to my next-door neighbour. "Not sleeping. Last night …"

But Mrs Kay didn't let me finish. "What about Amy? I hope you're making sure she gets some rest. Being a new mother is so difficult."

"I've left her asleep but I've got to get to work."

"I know you'll do your bit when you come home." She leaned over the fence and patted my arm.

Ben was beginning to whimper when I went back upstairs to find a tie without a baby sick stain. I picked him up and sniffed his bottom. Amy was still snoring. I glanced at my watch - there was just time for me to do the honours.

As I lay Ben on the changing-mat the phone rang.

"Hello. It's Sue, the Health Visitor. How's Ben today?"

"He's fine," I said, cocking my head to one side and slotting the telephone handset between my ear and shoulder. I needed two free hands to simultaneously clean Ben's bottom and stop him wriggling off the changing table.

"And how's Mum?"

I bristled with annoyance. Why didn't health professionals call Amy by her name? She was now 'Mum' and had been elevated to a pedestal far above me.

"You are looking after her aren't you, Andrew?"

"Yes." Now it was time for the lecture I'd been hearing from all and sundry since before Ben was even born.

"You must do your bit," she went on. "When Mum's been with baby all day she needs a break. Bath him when you get home from work and then cook the tea whilst Mum puts her feet up. Give her a chunk of 'me' time. She might appreciate a snooze in preparation for another sleepless night."

I resisted the urge to retort, "What about my sleep!"

How I longed to put my head on the pillow, snuggle under the duvet and close my eyes … I'd been up at least twice every night for the past four weeks changing nappies and supporting Amy as she got used to breastfeeding. I was fed up of listening to lectures that made me feel two inches high.

The phone rang again. Staring at Ben's innocent little face as he dropped back to sleep in his cot, I suppressed a swear word. If I answered the call I'd be late for work but if I let it ring it would wake either

Amy or Ben.

"Andrew, it's your father."

"Oh!"

Dad never rang. He left all domestic trivia to Mum.

"Your mother's gone to early morning yoga. I thought it was time for a man-to-man chat."

"A bit late for the birds and the bees, isn't it?"

"It's not that - I need to tell you about the Fathers' Club."

"No. I am not going to any class where health professionals are going to make me feel even more useless and unhelpful."

"You don't understand. It's all fathers together - we support each other. Uncle Reg introduced me just after you were born. It's a lifesaver."

"I don't want any more lessons in changing nappies, mixing bottles or supporting the hallowed person who gave birth - even though I love her very much. I want someone to notice me! All everyone sees is Amy and Ben. But I'm scuttling around like a mad thing in the background trying to keep everything afloat and earn money to pay the bills."

My sudden outpouring shocked me - Dad and me usually only discussed the football results. I must be more tired than I thought.

"Exactly! We meet every Friday at 7pm at the Black Horse."

"You can't do baby things in a pub."

"That's the whole point - we don't do baby things. You young ones escape all that baby stuff for a few hours and we oldies remind you how to enjoy yourselves."

"But you said Fathers' Club."

"We're all fathers - that's what we've got in common."

Suddenly I wasn't alone in a sea of tiredness and responsibility - Dad was throwing me a lifebelt.

"You're on," I said, "if I can keep my eyes open!"

MAKING NEWS

"Make it good! This is my last edition and I want to leave on a high." Steve, the editor of The Daily Record, placed a page of notes on Wayne's desk. "I want the chairman of the company to realise what a great leader he's losing in me."

Wayne took the A4 hand-written sheet from his boss. It was the big local story of the week and he didn't need the notes - he already knew the whole thing. It was an excellent story to go out on and Wayne couldn't help feeling envious.

"All this upheaval is tough on you, son, I know, especially as you've only been here a couple of weeks." Steve's voice lost its aggression. "I'll fetch you a coffee from that new place across the road whilst you get started."

"Thanks - a chocolate muffin would go down a treat as well." It was a long time since breakfast and Wayne's stomach was rumbling. He reached into his trouser pocket for some change.

"No need. This is on me, lad. It's the least I can do. And you're invited to the leaving party on Friday - drinks on the house."

"Thanks."

Wayne turned to his computer screen and started typing up the story. It had broken on Friday night, too late for the Saturday paper and The Daily Record didn't appear on Sundays.

Joshua, the other trainee reporter, had texted him with the news. At first Wayne hadn't believed it so he'd checked on the internet. No names were mentioned in the brief report he'd found there but it specifically mentioned a newsagent in the Thistlegate area of Moorhampton and so it had to be true.

Now he knew that it definitely was - this Monday morning the office was full of adrenaline and anticipation.

"I was going to give the story to Joshua to write." Steve was back with the coffee and cake. "He could've written it from the heart and given it some extra sparkle. But he hasn't turned up today. I don't blame him - given everything that's going on."

Joshua had joined the paper a couple of months before Wayne and was, therefore, higher in the pecking order when it came to the allocation of work. Joshua got sent to cover proper events like school speech days and swimming galas. Until now Wayne had been stringing stories together from the badly worded reports sent in by the enthusiastic but verbose secretaries of the Dahlia Society and the Women's Afternoon Club.

Wayne took a sip of the hot coffee and wished his boss would go away. It was hard to work with someone looking over his shoulder.

He was pleased that Joshua hadn't come in today. His fellow reporter would have done nothing but brag about what he and his fiancée, Sharon, were planning. He'd already texted Wayne that they were bringing the wedding forward and would set a new date just as soon as they'd found a house. That wouldn't take long because that's where he was today - house-hunting at the new development on the other side of town. Wayne wished he could afford to buy a house or even a tiny flat.

"I need that story in an hour," Steve said. "Then the chairman's coming in for an emergency meeting. You're invited."

"Me?"

"Yes. If you play your cards right there could be a promotion in this for you. I'm guessing you could become Senior Reporter."

Despite his low spirits, Wayne puffed up his chest. To be promoted to Senior Reporter after only two weeks in the job would be a significant achievement. Such a rapid promotion might even get him his dream job in Fleet Street before too long!

Now it was time to write the best story he could to ensure that promised elevation came his way - he didn't want some outsider brought in above him. This report wouldn't be too difficult and Joshua was sure to help out by texting him some pithy quotes where necessary.

Wayne started with the basics of the story as he'd been taught at college - Who? What? Where? When? Why? How? All the facts were at his fingertips he just had to string them together in an entertaining way. Pictures might be a problem. He could use the mug shots that were on file but they didn't convey the emotion and drama of what had happened.

"What about photos?" he called to Steve. "Will there be a press conference?"

"It's in a couple of days. Stick James Thornton's photo in for now. It's on file. He's the organiser. He flew back from a fortnight in Spain on Saturday - that's why you haven't bumped into him yet. He'd have definitely made himself known to you otherwise - it's a crying shame about that. Give him a call on his mobile and get a direct quote. And ask him from me where he's going for his next holiday." Steve passed Wayne a scrap of paper with a phone number on it.

Wayne finished writing the story with a couple of minutes to spare.

The meeting with the chairman was held in the editor's tiny office. Steve brought in more coffees from the new shop and some posh sandwiches wrapped in cellophane.

"I may as well go out in style," he said plonking a selection of miniature sugar packets and some sticky 'Millionaire's Shortbread' on the table as well.

The chairman didn't smile. "All this is rather sudden and it's causing us problems at head office. We appreciate you sticking around to get today's issue out but I'm here to persuade you to stay a bit longer. Your contract states three months' notice. We'd like you to honour it."

Steve shook his head. "This time last week I was just a faceless number on your payroll. I got sent meaningless directive after meaningless directive. I was expected to work overtime almost daily with no extra payment. My wife left me because she never saw me and now I never see my kids. This is my chance to make it up to them and mend my family. I've got the money to treat them and I don't feel guilty about jacking in my job and taking the time to be with them."

The chairman looked shell-shocked. Wayne decided to seize his chance.

"Sir," he said. "I'm one of the reporters on the team here. I'm keen to make The Daily Record one of the best local papers around. Is there anything I can do to help fill the gap?"

"The problem is rather bigger than just an editor walking out." The chairman eyed Wayne up and down. "I have a mass resignation on my hands. Every single employee of this newspaper is leaving without notice, except you. Why aren't you going too?"

"I wasn't in the syndicate yet. I've only been here two …"

"Wayne's very experienced," Steve cut in. "He's written up an excellent story this morning. I'd like to recommend him for promotion to senior reporter." Then he placed the report in front of the chairman.

"Thistlegate Daily Record Syndicate Wins Euro Millions!"

SALVATION BY IAIN PATTISON

Iain and I 'swapped' stories when we were both compiling collections for publication. We hope this introduces a new writer to our readers. Iain is a humourist, full-time author, creative writing tutor and competition judge. Find out more about him at www.iainpattison.com.

The frail woman's eyes fluttered open, and she coughed harshly, spasms rocking her body.

For a moment Michael thought she might not see him, like all the others who'd failed to notice his slow, graceful passage through the many wretched wards of the Chicago hospital. But she smiled weakly, hand reaching out.

"I've been expecting you," she whispered, lips dry. "I knew I wasn't getting any better, no matter what those fool doctors said. It's my time, isn't it?"

He shook his head, smiling back. "No, Martha. Not yet. Not for many years to come."

Her look was disbelieving. "Then why has an angel appeared at my bedside?"

It was impossible not to be impressed. Even in her emaciated and exhausted state, Martha had identified him for what he was - although he had no mythical wings, halo or blinding brilliance; and was dressed in an ordinary business suit.

They were right, he told himself, she was extraordinary; unquestionably worth his divine intervention.

"I've come to restore you to health," he replied. "To share my precious life force with you."

If her instant recognition of his celestial countenance had surprised him, her next words left Michael completely stunned.

"Why me?" she croaked. "Why, out of everyone in this terrible place, are you saving me?"

He considered her spotless soul, her unwavering belief, the fund-raising dinners she'd hosted for the cathedral restoration project and the cash given willingly to help those suffering in disaster zones around the globe. She was, he mused, the rarest of all creatures - a good person in a cruel and callous world.

A sudden alarm outside broke his train of thought, as did the tense voices and the clatter of the emergency cart that sped past the closed doors of the private room.

"What's that?" she asked, trying to raise her head.

"It's nothing to concern you," he replied, pushing the commotion from his consciousness. "It's simply a death. One of many that will occur here tonight. It's routine."

"Who is it? Who is dying?"

Michael closed his eyes and visualised the scene at

the far end of the ward... the crash team fighting to restart the young man's stalled heart... the nurse yelling "stand clear" as the electric paddles made contact with the youth's heavily tattooed chest... the doctor administering the adrenaline injection... and the distraught face of the dying boy's mother, collapsing to the floor, writhing in torment, screeching in a despair beyond words.

"No-one of consequence," he answered, focusing back on Martha. "A gang member, a hoodlum. He's about to expire from bullet wounds. He was shot by the store owner he was attempting to rob."

"How old is he?" she asked.

"Fifteen," he replied, adding: "A short life, but that's nothing unusual for his kind."

He went to place his healing hand on her clammy forehead, but she grabbed his wrist. The grip was surprisingly strong.

"His kind? No-one of consequence?" she hissed. "That's not the way an angel should speak. He may be a hoodlum but he's a person like anyone else; someone with a soul. Tell me about him – this child you're writing off."

Michael made a pained face. "I promise you there is nothing remarkable about Ramon. He was brought up in the projects, his drunken father walked out when he was a baby and his mother had to work three jobs to support the family.

"He ran wild on the streets, stealing by the age of eight, taking automobiles at 10 and was enrolled into the Bloods not much later. Since then there has been nothing but drug dealing, petty crime, feuds, drinking and intimidation. His life has been a waste, a blight on others."

He pushed his hand down towards her, but Martha's grip tightened.

"I want you to save him," she instructed.

"What!"

"Save him," she repeated. "You can do it. You're an angel. You've got the power."

Why, he demanded, bemused.

"Because Ramon had no choice but to be what he was. He never had a chance, doomed from the beginning."

Martha flicked her eyes around the private room, at the plasma TV, the soft bedding and subdued lighting, at the state-of-the-art medical equipment.

"I'm rich," she said. "And it's easy to be good when you've got cash. It's easy to make the right choices when all it takes is signing a blank cheque."

Michael looked deep into her determined eyes. "There's nothing to say that the boy won't continue just the way he was; go back to his wicked existence and cause more harm and pain."

"Yes," she conceded, "but at least he'll have a choice this time. Maybe he'll change. Who's to say? Everyone deserves one chance at salvation."

Her line of reasoning was remarkably persuasive, however Michael hadn't told her everything.

"I can save only one person tonight," he announced. "I have only enough life force for one. If he lives, you will die."

Her instant nod was all he needed to know.

No-one saw Michael as he walked silently along the ward and, leaning over Ramon, touched the young man's motionless chest. The heart monitor bleeped back into action, to gasps of disbelief.

As he turned, Michael heard a woman sobbing

hysterically: "He's going to live. Oh Lord, oh Lord, my baby's going to live. Thank you, merciful God. Thank you."

Heading back towards Martha's room, he marvelled. Humans were such a toxic mixture of greed, prejudice, deceit, violence, and lust. Yet every so often one small act of compassion, a selfless sacrifice, meant none of that mattered.

Tonight Martha's kindness had taught him that maybe, for all its flaws, mankind deserved a second chance, a shot at redemption.

She was waiting for him, at the swirling vortex, her spirit ready to step through.

"Was this a test of my faith?" she asked.

Wiping away a silvery tear, the angel shook his head.

"No," he said with a new humbled certainty. "It was a test of mine."

***

Birmingham-based Iain Pattison has been entertaining readers on both sides of the Atlantic for more than 15 years with a succession of short stories that have won prize after prize, appeared in magazines and anthologies, and been broadcast on the UK's most prestigious speech radio station, BBC Radio 4.

His work spans everything from romance to historical fantasy, humour to gothic horror, and when not penning twist-ender tales, he is a creative writing tutor, competition judge and public speaker.

To learn more about Iain follow him on Twitter @AuthorIain or visit iainpattison.com.

TOO FAST, TOO SOON

I ring the doorbell and wait for Maxine to answer. It's Valentine's Day and we haven't spoken for a month. I've brought a peace offering tied up in red ribbon.

The split was my fault.

Back when we met, I was happy to take things at her pace. She said that rushing never worked.

"Neither of us wants to get hurt," she said and gave an impish grin.

I fell for that smile.

We had a routine. Maxine picked me up from work three times a week and that period alone together, before she dropped me off at home, became precious.

"I think you're using me to save on bus fares," she said once, her eyes wide and flirtatious.

That was the first time I kissed her. There was only a moment's hesitation before she kissed me back. After that we started seeing each other more often.

We would walk to the pub so that we could both enjoy a drink. Maxine couldn't risk putting her licence on the line and I was still using 'L' plates.

But after a while I got frustrated with how things were progressing. She knew I wanted to speed things up.

"It's too soon, Paul," she said.

"Maxine, it's been weeks now. Surely it wouldn't hurt. My mate made more progress in just a fortnight with his …"

"He probably indulged in one night stands as well," she snapped. "Everyone's different and I don't want to hear about the antics of your friend."

Questioning Maxine's judgement like that was a big mistake.

Now I stare at her door and cross my fingers that she can forgive. Perhaps she's seen me from the window and decided not to answer. I look at the beribboned package and think I should've got flowers as well.

After our disagreement I tried to put things right with red roses. I didn't want to lose Maxine.

"I love you," I said.

She placed them gently in the back seat of the car. "I've been thinking too. I'm ready, if you're sure it's what you want."

She looked uncomfortable and I could tell it wasn't what she really wanted. I leant over and kissed her gently. Her usual ardour was missing.

"We both have to be in agreement about this," I said. "If you don't think we're ready then we'll leave it for another time."

"I'm worried about your confidence. If we do it and then I have to stop you halfway, it could be disastrous. I should never have let our relationship get this far."

"So, do you want me to find someone else?"

"Yes. No. I mean I don't know. Let's do it once and see how we go."

Now I can hear footsteps in the hall. My stomach flips and I hope I've judged this right.

Four weeks ago forcing Maxine to go further than she wanted didn't go well.

The main road into town was busy. It was rush hour and there were hazards everywhere; people stepping onto zebra crossings, cars pulling out of side roads and then those unexpected temporary traffic lights.

"Brake!" Maxine shouted.

My foot hit the pedal and I realised she'd already pressed the dual controls. As we nudged the car in front we'd slowed to a walking pace.

She dealt with the fallout from the other driver.

"There's no damage," she said as he finally drove away. "But I would never have allowed an ordinary pupil with your lack of ability out on this road."

When we arrived back at my house there were tears in her eyes. "Please don't contact me again - either as your driving instructor or your girlfriend. Getting involved with a pupil was a big mistake."

The light went out of my life.

Now Maxine is standing in the doorway before me.

I hand her the package. She unties the ribbon and opens the envelope to reveal a red and pink Valentine card declaring my love for her. It also contains my 'Pass' certificate.

"I paid for an intensive course. Can we

concentrate on just the personal relationship now?"

She nods and that impish smile plays across her face. "Who'll be in the driving seat?" she asks.

"I thought we'd stick with dual controls."

RESCUE!

Malcolm shielded his eyes and stared up at the lone figure. She was at the top, silhouetted against the setting sun. Her terrified calls for help had subsided but they would erupt again if the weather worsened. The sky looked heavy and more snow was forecast. Malcolm crossed his fingers.

Caroline was brave and loved a challenge but everyone had their limits and it seemed Caroline had just reached hers. He remembered his own fear when, as a younger man, he winter climbed for the first time in the Highlands. Like Caroline today, that expedition had included the longest ascent he'd ever done.

"Reach to the left, Caroline!" he called.

She moved slightly and then wobbled with one arm flailing wildly, searching unsuccessfully for a handhold. It was obvious the climb had worn her out both physically and mentally. Now she was unable to retrace her steps, frozen both by the weather and fear.

Despite the nagging ache in his hip, Malcolm would have to go to her aid - any other help would take too long to arrive. He reached above his head, gripped hard and then felt for a foothold. Everywhere was coated with a thin layer of ice and it was difficult to get a secure grasp of anything. He lifted an arm and looked up to seek the next handhold. Suddenly his right foot lost contact with the slippery frost and shot from under him. Malcolm was left hanging by one arm and one leg. His hip shrieked with unexpected pain. For a second his free limbs waved and kicked before making contact with something solid. He steadied himself and took a few deep breaths.

"Help!" Caroline called. "I can't move!"

"I'm nearly there." Malcolm hoped he sounded calmer than he felt.

"It's getting dark!" Her frightened voice was like a cat's mew.

This foolhardy predicament was Malcolm's fault. When Caroline had suggested going climbing he'd checked the weather forecast. Snow and high winds were expected and he'd said no. The Scottish weather was always unpredictable and Caroline didn't have enough climbing experience to cope with bad conditions.

"But in two days' time I go back to London," she'd pleaded. "There's nothing as exciting as this there. Everything is much bigger here."

Malcolm understood what she meant. Even on his short visits he found London claustrophobic and grubby. Everyone lived on top of one another and it was impossible to escape from other people. There were plenty of green spaces in the parks but there was always a jogger or cyclist to negotiate and the playgrounds were swarming with children. Scotland was a much better place for those who loved the outdoors, like him and Caroline.

"Alright, I'll take you climbing." Against his better judgement he'd given in to her pleas. "But we'll have to go prepared for bad weather."

"Yes!" She'd raised her fist in the air triumphantly.

The cold was seeping through Malcom's gloves now; they weren't thick enough for clutching at ice. Before long his hands would be too numb to grip properly. Caroline was still out of reach. Every time the wind blew, her long blonde hair reared up and whipped across her face. When she'd started the climb she'd been wearing a snug-fitting thermal hat but somewhere along the way it had been lost to the elements.

"Are you OK, Caroline?" He yelled but the wind grabbed his words and tossed them away. He didn't know if she'd heard him. "Are you OK!"

Her head moved from side to side and she opened her mouth. He couldn't hear what she said. The dropping temperature might cause her to slip and crash all the way to the bottom. He should call for help. But his mobile was in the pocket of his Puffa jacket and there was no way he could get it out and make a call whilst clinging on to his handholds. If he did manage to get the phone out of his pocket without falling, there might not be any signal - in this area it came and went in an unpredictable fashion. There was no choice but to plough on. He reached out with his leg to lever himself further up and his hip complained again.

Earlier he'd packed the rucksack with a flask of hot chocolate and sandwiches. There was a first aid kit too but unfortunately the insulated silver blanket he'd used on expeditions had gone missing. He'd also stuffed in some emergency Kendal Mint Cake and a couple of bananas for instant energy. These provisions hadn't gone unnoticed by Caroline and the mint cake had all been eaten by the time she'd finished warming up on smaller climbs, ready for this big one. At least he still had the hot drink to warm her.

The rucksack was hampering his climb. It made his body bulky and got caught on overhangs. With hindsight he should have taken it off before attempting this rescue. When he got to Caroline it would be impossible to balance, manipulate the flask and pour her a drink.

"I'm so cold!" Caroline's weak voice drifted down to him. "I think my feet have died."

"Wriggle your toes!" commanded Malcolm. "And let's sing. That will make us feel better." He started with the first song that came into his head from his Navy days. "For those in peril on the sea!" Immediately he realised it wasn't quite as jolly and warming as they needed and switched. "What shall we do with the drunken sailor? What shall we do with the drunken sailor early in the morning?"

There was no sign of Caroline joining in. Malcolm sang louder so that she could be in no doubt that he was nearly with her.

His mind wandered to his wife. Dorothy would be home from the shops by now. He'd left a note to say where they'd gone but she'd be worried – in a few minutes it would be completely dark and, without the sun, the temperature was plummeting. He wondered how long she'd leave it before raising the alarm or trying to look for them herself.

Malcolm's outstretched hand touched Caroline's boots. It took only a couple more reaches and pulls and he was perched beside her at the top.

"Granddad!" she exclaimed. "It's dark, slippery and cold. How are we going to get back down?"

"Slowly but surely," he said, putting his free arm around her shoulders and trying to transfer some of his body warmth.

"Look, lights!"

Malcolm followed her gaze below them. Torch beams were piercing the darkness. There were voices too, getting louder as the lights got nearer.

"Caroline adores climbing. She's only six but has the agility of a cat." It was Dorothy speaking. "She wanted to conquer the big climbing frame here in the park before going back to her parents in London." The wind had dropped and her words were clear. "My husband was foolish enough to bring her this afternoon despite the weather warnings. I called you because Malcom's had a hip replacement. If Caroline got stuck he wouldn't have been much use."

The torchlight was pointed upwards and two firemen surged up the climbing frame to rescue them.

THE KEY OF THE DOOR

Shortlisted in Writers' News 'Pride and Prejudice' Competition

Mother was in full dictatorial flow. From her bedroom, Anne could hear the scolded caterers scuttling around the kitchen, like ants rudely unearthed from their nest.

"Yes, Mrs de Bourgh. Of course, Mrs de Bourgh." They were sycophants to their temporary employer.

Mother always thought she knew better than everyone else – even professionals trying to do their job.

Going downstairs now would only cause more maternal outrage because Anne wasn't wearing the outfit that Mother had chosen for tonight.

That was a scarlet, strapless, full length gown, twinkling with a thousand sequins – and totally impractical for what lay ahead.

"The birthday girl must stand out from her guests," Mother had gushed, as their Harrods' personal shopper tried to side with Anne's request for something less showy. "Everyone will be looking at you, darling."

Inevitably Mother got her way, just as she had about every aspect of tonight's party.

Anne didn't want a twenty-first birthday party at all. She'd argued for an evening at the pub with her few close friends. But Mother had insisted on this over the top 'do'.

"It will be a wonderful opportunity to showcase you," she'd enthused, "and maybe you and Fitzwilliam will get a little closer!"

Anne knew that trying to snare Fitz Darcy was a pointless exercise – why should one of the wealthiest men in London fancy her?

And even if he did, Anne didn't like him, let alone want a long-term relationship with him. Granted, he was text book handsome with dark wavy hair and brown sultry eyes – like the hero of a Sunday night period drama. But he never smiled, at least not with his eyes and he barely spoke, unless asked a direct question. Fitzwilliam Darcy was rude, obnoxious and arrogant – the complete opposite of Jed from the art gallery.

Mother disapproved of Jed.

The thought of going downstairs now was tying Anne's stomach in knots. She took another sip of the Champagne that her mother had brought up earlier and wished it was something stronger.

"Are you ready, Anne, dear? Your guests will be arriving soon."

The caterers must be in earshot because Mother

was using her best telephone voice as she tapped on the bedroom door.

Anne re-applied her lipstick, which had transferred itself to the Champagne glass. The rest of her thick make-up was still perfect. Anne hated the way it clung to her pores. She longed to wash it all off and go bare-skinned, however Mother wouldn't countenance that and, to be sure, she'd checked Anne's make-up just before the caterers had arrived.

"How will you ever snare Fitzwilliam with such a pale, plain face as yours?" Mother had said when she'd first decided on her daughter's future husband. "A little bit of war paint never did anyone any harm and it can only do you good."

Then she'd packed Anne off to the Ladies' Beauty Academy for lessons in how to give herself the 'perfect' face.

Fitzwilliam Darcy was a distant relative on Mother's side of the family and he was wealthy with a capital 'W'. His father had bought him a penthouse in Canary Wharf when he landed a job with a top merchant bank after graduating with first class honours in PPE from Oxford.

That was when Mother had decided that they too should live in London's Docklands.

"After all, that's where all the eligible men are," she'd said and then winked before adding, "especially the one we've got our eye on."

Anne had tried to explain that London didn't interest her - she wanted to study for a degree in Library Studies at the local university and then make books her career.

"Certainly not!" Mother wouldn't listen. "How will you ever find a husband with your nose in a book?

It's much better to get a man who will pull you up the social scale so that you have no need to work. And once you've snared him, make sure he's well insured – then if he should keel over with a heart attack, like your father, you won't suffer at all."

So Mother had wangled Anne a job as a receptionist in a private art gallery owned by a friend.

"You'll meet the right sort of people there. And you'll get a say in the guest list for private view events – make sure that you always include Fitzwilliam. The more familiar you become to him, the more likely he is to take the initiative. Before you know it, you two will be an item!"

As usual Anne had followed orders and her distant cousin had attended several of these occasions. Mother said that this was a sign that things were progressing nicely and that before long he'd be asking her out to dinner.

"You're developing a common interest – the love of art. You'll have lots to talk about."

Anne knew differently. At each private view, Fitz had barely spoken two words to her, apart from thanking her for the invitation, preferring instead to talk to Charles Bingley, the male friend that he always brought along with him. Jed was the one who'd kept her company as she organised drinks and canapés for the guests. In fact these days he was the only one who kept her sane.

"Anne! They're starting to arrive." The tapping on the bedroom door had become a loud knock.

Anne looked in the mirror. Her cheeks were flushed – was that too much blusher, too much Champagne or plain excitement about her future? In her black patent clutch bag were the left luggage tickets for the suitcase and rucksack she'd deposited at King's Cross the previous day. She picked up her mobile and then decided it belonged with her old life. She dropped it into the toilet bowl and it made a satisfying splash. A plague of calls and texts from Mother was the last thing she wanted.

Anne took a deep breath and went downstairs to the hall. Pink and white helium balloons emblazoned with '21' bobbed on silver ribbons and vases of pink and white roses rested on every surface. Anne's birthday cards were placed ostentatiously where they could be seen. Mother was anxious to make her daughter look popular but, in reality, the majority were from relatives and her own acquaintances.

"Here's the birthday girl!" announced one of Mother's middle-aged cronies, pointing towards Anne on the staircase. "Hasn't she grown? I remember when she was nothing but a twinkle in her father's eye."

Anne greeted the older woman who was in London especially for the party. For once Mother didn't say a word but Anne could feel her unspoken criticism as she looked her daughter up and down.

As soon as politeness would allow, Mother directed the woman towards a uniformed waitress balancing a tray of glasses and then she dragged Anne by the arm into a quiet corner.

"Where is the red dress?" she hissed. "You look like you're going to a funeral instead of your own birthday party."

Anne glanced down at her favourite black trouser suit. She'd added a crimson silk blouse and a crystal brooch in the shape of an owl to jazz things up a bit.

"The dress wasn't very practical for what I'm

planning."

"What are you talking about?" Mother raised her hand towards Anne's cheek, as if to slap her.

"Mrs de Bourgh," called the hired butler as he went to answer the front door. "Your presence is required."

Mother had to satisfy herself with a low volume snarl at Anne before slipping on her hostess smile and greeting the guests who were now handing their coats to the butler.

Darcy arrived next with Charles Bingley.

"Fitzwilliam! I'm so glad you could make it." Mother sounded like she would prostrate herself at Darcy's feet and lick his shoes if protocol would allow. "Anne has told me all about your interest in art."

Darcy spoke no more than a couple of words and merely nodded a greeting towards Anne but Charles stepped forward and shook her hand warmly. "Happy Birthday!"

It was the first sincere greeting Anne had received all day and she nearly burst into tears. But now was not the time for losing control – the best was yet to come. She continued to meet and greet under Mother's disapproving eye. Small talk with people she barely knew was hard work – these were Mother's kind of people, not hers. Then Jed arrived.

He was in charge of PR and marketing at the gallery. He kissed her on the lips and then gave her a hug.

"OK, Sweetie?"

She nodded.

"Good evening, Gerard," Mother said coldly.

They'd rowed about his inclusion on the guest list.

"That friend of yours is nothing but a jumped up grammar school boy with no background," she'd said after Anne had tried to tell her how kind Jed was. "He's not a proper gentleman, unlike Fitzwilliam."

Now the dining room was cauldron of conversation. With Jed at her side, Anne banged her wine glass with a spoon to attract attention.

A chorus of "Shush" went round the room like a Mexican wave. Anne's mother glared.

"Ladies and Gentleman," Anne began, nerves threatening to steal her voice. "I have an announcement."

Mother looked close to an explosion at this unscheduled interruption to the carefully planned evening.

"Jed and I are leaving London. Now."

Mother was pushing through the guests towards them. There was the sound of a taxi horn outside.

"I will be studying Librarianship and Jed has a job with a new gallery. Please have another drink and the buffet will be served shortly."

Anne grabbed Jed's hand and they headed for the front door. Mother caught them in the hallway.

"What about Fitzwilliam? What's happening?"

"I won't be manipulated into the arms of someone who thinks only of himself." Anne was growing in confidence now. "Jed isn't rich but we love each other and that makes us wealthy in the most important way."

Then she pushed something into her mother's hand. "I don't need this anymore."

It was her front door key.

LAST BUS HOME

The girls spilled out of the pub in a rainbow of bright tops, snug jeans and high heels. The man in the car pulled his balaclava down over his face. He watched the women cluster in the pooling light of a street lamp.

"Where is she?" he muttered impatiently.

Excited female squeals and shouts rose above the drone of the late night traffic. His window slid silently open and he listened for her familiar voice, trying to discover if she was there amongst them. It would be easier if he knew what she was wearing.

"Those lads from the pub are over there!" giggled one high-pitched voice. "Look, Suzette!"

Sitting in the car he felt himself both tense and relax at the mention of her name. She was here! He was outside the right pub at the right time. He tried to slither further behind the steering wheel and out of the glow of the street lights.

"It's the one that fancied you, Suzette, the one with the cute smile."

The man sat up straight and tried to spot the other male that was encroaching on his territory. A group of young men stood half in and half out of the pub waving at the girls.

"Tattooed gorillas," muttered the male in the car. The thought of one of these lads going near Suzette turned his stomach.

"You left this inside."

He watched a youth with snake hips hand something small and black to Suzette.

"My mobile! Thanks."

The man in the car winced as Suzette gave her benefactor a dazzling smile. She pocketed the phone without her eyes ever leaving the young man's face. He returned her gaze and then leant forward slightly. For an awful second, the man in the car thought the lad was going to kiss Suzette but at the last moment he stepped back and returned to his friends.

"Here's the bus!" yelled a woman with sequins emblazoned across her T-shirt.

"Thank goodness," muttered the man. Once Suzette was on the bus there would be no danger of her spotting him. When she got off she'd be alone and he knew exactly how he would play it then. She wouldn't kick up a fuss.

He wondered if his wife had missed him yet. He'd said something to her about watching the match with Dave but she'd been too engrossed in the beeps of a life-support machine on *Casualty* to take any notice.

The bus pulled up just behind his car and the man stared into his rear-view mirror to check Suzette got on. But the driver switched off the engine and stepped onto the pavement. He cupped his hand, struck a match and lit a cigarette. The man in the car drummed his fingers impatiently - surely the bus driver wanted to finish the night's work just as much as he himself did.

"That car's been parked there a long time." The female voice floated in through the open window.

Balaclava'd lips silently urged the smoking bus driver to finish his cigarette and get on his way.

"I bet he's up to no good." It was sequin woman again. "Shall we get one of the lads to move him on?"

Two of the tattooed gorillas broke from the group and moved towards the car, immediately the driver started the engine and pulled away. The next bus stop was only a couple of minutes away and there was a secluded side road on which to park. He'd checked it out the previous day to allow for small hiccups to his plan.

So far he was sure Suzette hadn't seen him. He was driving a courtesy car lent to him by the garage that morning so neither she nor any of her friends would recognise it from the school car park.

In the lane he did a three-point turn and switched off the headlights but he left the engine running. If he got too far behind the bus Suzette might disappear before he reached her.

Then the bus came into view and it sailed straight past the stop. The man had to pull out quickly to avoid losing it. Then he swore as blue lights danced behind him. Suddenly remembering the balaclava he tore it off and tossed it into the darkness of the passenger foot-well. If the police pulled him over it wouldn't be wise to be dressed as a bank robber.

Sure enough they indicated that he should stop the

car. He breathed deeply and tried to look innocent – after all he'd done nothing wrong.

"Good evening, Sir. Did you know your near-side rear light isn't working?"

"No, I'm sorry I didn't. It's a courtesy car and I'll report it when I take it back." He was talking too fast but he wanted to get rid of the policeman and back on the tail of the bus.

"Have you been drinking, Sir?" The policeman appeared to sniff the air.

"No." After his previous conviction he had learned not to draw the police's attention to himself.

The bus disappeared from view.

"Thank you, Sir." The policeman nodded a farewell and retreated to his own car.

The man gingerly pulled back out into the traffic. He stuck rigidly to the speed limit in case the blue lights appeared again. As a teacher he didn't want to risk them feeding his details into their computer.

Suddenly the bus was in front of him sitting in a lay-by disgorging passengers. He had no choice but to go past it and pull in a hundred yards down the road.

Several of the beautiful butterflies and illustrated apes were heading for a chip shop. Suzette must be almost alone on the bus now with only two stops left. She was an easy target. He wondered if there was CCTV on there and whether the cameras were loaded with film. He weighed up the risk of letting her finish the bus journey or moving in now and causing a public scene. He thought of her sitting there alone and couldn't wait any longer. He opened the car door and ran towards the bus. It pulled away just before he reached it forcing him to sprint back to his car.

No-one got off at the next stop but a gang of

leather-jacketed youths boarded. They were going to get to Suzette before him. She was young and beautiful but still only a child. What chance would she have against yobs like that? He thumped the dashboard in anguish.

Suzette got off at the next stop. Alone. Now she was his. The bus pulled away and she started walking. She looked fragile and vulnerable away from the crowd. Her high heels made her walk slowly and awkwardly. She wouldn't be able to run.

He pulled up alongside her, pressing the button to open the passenger window. "Fancy a lift?" he called.

"Dad! You promised you'd trust me to get the bus."

"I was just passing."

Suzette rolled her eyes with disbelief as she climbed into the car. "Coming home on the last bus is perfectly safe," she said. "I'm not waiting there all alone. Tonight the lads scared off some weirdo in a balaclava."

THE WORM TEST

"I wasn't going to tell you this," James glanced quickly over his shoulder to check that his daughter was still safely plugged into her iPod on the back seat of the car. "Emily suggested this Worm's Head excursion as a test for you."

"A test?" I repeated.

"She's been reading some book or other, 'The Stepmother Challenges', I think it's called. The heroine sets a series of challenges for the woman about to become her stepmother."

"But I'm not about to become her stepmother, am I?"

James and I had been seeing each other for the past ten months but there'd been no mention of marriage. He'd joined one of the salsa classes that I teach and I'd danced with him a lot in those first few weeks in order to get him up to speed with the others. Then he took me out to dinner. I fell head over heels in love but James insisted on taking things slowly.

"I think Emily's playing it safe, just in case," James said. "Besides, you never know what the future might bring." He threw me a wink and my stomach somersaulted with possibilities.

This was only the fourth time that 10-year-old Emily and I had met. Despite my pleas, James had refused to introduce us until he was sure that our relationship was going to last.

"Susannah, you have to understand," he'd explained. "It's been just me and Emily since her mum died 9 years ago. I have to be careful."

Inevitably our first meeting had been awkward. We'd gone to Emily's favourite pizza restaurant and the conversation had been stilted but James reported back that Emily thought I was 'OK'. Things improved on our subsequent afternoons out bowling and to the cinema. James has done a great job bringing Emily up alone and I felt like a real friendship was growing between his daughter and me. But this sudden mention of a 'test' seemed to be a backward step. Had I done something wrong?

"No, nothing wrong," James said. "We often come here with my two brothers and their families. I think Emily's worried that if you won't make the crossing to Worm's Head then we'll have to stop those days out. Emily's a real tomboy – probably because all her cousins are boys and a few years older than her. One of them had a girlfriend who refused to go across and completely ruined that day's outing."

"I better not let her down then."

"Don't worry, it's not too difficult." James pulled into a cliff top car park. "At low tide we take the causeway out to Worm's Head, climb the hill and then come back."

Even to a confirmed city dweller like me, that didn't sound too difficult.

We pulled on our waterproofs against the blowy, wet weather. Not used to the great outdoors, I'd borrowed an old one from James. Emily set off in front of us, leading the way along the coast path, past the National Trust gift shop and towards an island sitting off shore a short distance away. As we followed, James took my hand then let it go abruptly as Emily turned around – he wanted her to get to know me as his 'friend' before dropping the complication of romance into the mix. But I doubted Emily believed this 'friend' business – otherwise, why did she set a 'stepmother' challenge?

We veered off the path and across wet grass towards a small, stone-built building with a free-standing 'Coastwatch' signboard swaying outside it. A few people were surveying the island through binoculars.

"Perfect," said James as we got near enough to read the tide times on the board. "The causeway is already open."

The wind had got stronger and was sending stinging drops of rain into my eyes. I would have preferred to spend the afternoon in a café with a mug of hot chocolate – but how difficult could it be to walk across to an island and back?

Emily stuffed her iPod away and told us to follow her. We passed another swaying sign on the path down to the causeway. In large letters it proclaimed, 'Deaths have occurred whilst crossing the flooded causeway'.

"We're safe, Susannah, the tide is out," James said,

sensing my fear.

The paved path ended in a three foot drop, down to the rocky causeway. Emily jumped lightly on to the stones. She looked up, expecting me to do the same.

"Aren't there any steps?" I asked. This wasn't going to be as easy as James had made out.

"Of course not!" Emily rolled her eyes. "If there were steps and a tarmac road between us and the Worm, it would be boring!"

So, the challenge began here and any wimpy behaviour on my part would earn an immediate 'fail' from Emily.

"I'll help you." James had already climbed down beside his daughter and was holding out his hand to assist me.

"It's fine," I lied and, crouching down, I managed to lower myself from the grass to the first of the rocks.

Emily set off, picking her way neatly over the rocks and, every so often, throwing a glance back at me. I glued on a smile and waved as much as I could without losing my balance. There was more water than I expected between us and Worm's Head. It was pooling around the boulders, waiting to soak those who chose the wrong, wobbly stone to hop on. James was close on the tail of his daughter. If I didn't start moving quickly I'd have to find my own way over the rocks instead of merely following the footsteps of those that had done it before.

I stepped out, wobbled and righted myself before jumping to the next rock that was sitting above the waterline. My arms were outstretched for balance and I kept my eyes glued to James' legs, memorising where he placed his feet. I was petrified of choosing a wobbly stone that would tip me into the water. Eventually, father and daughter stopped to investigate one of the pools and I caught up with them.

"You're doing fine," said James quietly and squeezed my hand as Emily's back was turned.

I wanted to keep hold of him for the rest of the crossing but I knew Emily wouldn't approve.

"Look at this crab!" Emily was using a wind-bleached stick to indicate the pink crustacean crouched under the water.

Its body was the size of a saucer and it had legs to match. The thought of the creature scuttling across the sand, reminded me of those terrible spiders which run around the bottom of the bath when the tap is turned on. Emily moved her stick nearer to the crab and prodded.

It sprinted. I screamed and a sudden gust of wind inflated my hood and waterproof. Caught off balance I sat down heavily in a pool of sea water.

"You look like the Michelin man!" laughed Emily, puffing up her cheeks and holding her arms slightly away from her body in an imitation of the tyre man.

"That's not a nice thing to say," said James, helping me up. "Apologise to Susannah, please, Emily."

"Sorry," said his daughter, staring at her feet.

"That's OK. I know I must look funny."

"We better call it a day," James said. "You're much too wet to carry on."

Then he gave Emily a look, which I interpreted as 'don't you dare whinge or moan'.

"A little bit of water never hurt anyone," I replied gaily and brushed myself down, not wanting to spoil Emily's day or fail the challenge. "We're over halfway, let's carry on."

I forced myself to take the lead for a while. The going was a bit easier now. The water and rocks had been replaced with a thick bed of dark blue and purple mussel shells that crunched underfoot. The cold wind was making my wet jeans feel like a covering of ice but I was buoyed up by the thought that I hadn't given in.

"We're here!" proclaimed Emily, racing ahead of me and climbing up onto the grassy bank of Worm's Head.

She stood by a sign with a brass bell hanging underneath it.

"If stranded, ring bell continuously to attract attention," I read aloud and shivered.

Given our distance from the mainland and the strength of the wind, I had serious doubts that the sound would reach anyone capable of helping a stranded walker.

"Now we climb the hill." Emily strode forward.

James motioned me to go next and, when his daughter wasn't looking, he placed his hand on my back and helped me up the steep slope with a push.

The top of the hill was completely exposed to the elements and I was itching to get home into dry clothes. But I renewed my smile and hopped around on the spot to keep warm. We all looked like Michelin men now with the wind finding its way into every nook and cranny of our waterproofs.

Looking down to the rocky causeway, I could see a steady stream of ant-like people leaving Worm's Head and heading back across to the mainland. The inadequate bell loomed large in my mind but, refusing to be a scaredy-cat, I said nothing about the impending return of the sea. James got his camera out and took pictures of Emily and I. Then Emily insisted on me taking endless photos of her with her father.

"Wow!" I said flicking through the results on the digital camera. "You two look really good together." I wanted her to know that I wasn't a threat to the bond between them.

Emily smiled and hung on her father's arm.

Finally we made our way back down the hillside, blackberry bushes tugging at our legs and making the going difficult.

Dusk was falling as we reached the start of the causeway, my heavy, damp jeans were making it harder and harder to walk and I was anxious – there was no bell for those stranded halfway across and deaths had occurred... But as we set off, I finally found my 'worm' balancing legs and, thankfully, Emily had lost interest in the contents of the rock pools. All the same, I felt an enormous relief as I climbed off the last rock and pulled myself up onto the paved path. I was past caring about getting muddy knees or dirt beneath my fingernails.

As we made our way back up the slope to the squat Coastwatch building Emily trailed behind James and me. I slowed down to walk with her.

"That was difficult," I said, "but worth it. It was a good idea of yours. Shall we help each other up this last bit of the hill?"

"You didn't do badly, Susannah, seeing as you got so wet." Emily put her hand in mine and I felt her tired weight pull on my arm.

Then we caught up with James.

"You can hold Susannah's hand too if you like, Daddy," Emily announced and then she turned to me. "Are you any good at skiing? We could go to the dry slope next time. I'm having lessons."

With James and Emily on either side of me, it looked like I'd passed the Worm Test and qualified to take stage 2 of Emily's challenges. She was facing her fear of sharing her father so it was only fair that I too made the occasional, scary leap into the unknown.

When James squeezed my hand I knew the result would be worth it.

HOUSE GUESTS

Dorothy pressed hard on her car horn for a second time. The neighbours' curtains twitched but there was still no response from her house.

Despite the descending gloom and the driving rain, Anthony was clearly visible, he was strutting his stuff in the brightly lit window of her lounge. Why did the young never bother to close the curtains? And how did they stand such loud music? Even at this distance and sealed in the car, she could feel the heavy bass beat.

Behind her grandson she could see another boy and there were a couple of girls in mini-skirts. They were twirling and dancing in the spotlight of her faux chandelier.

"I refuse to park in the road," Dorothy muttered to herself. "I have a perfectly good driveway. I am not carrying my shopping through the rain when I should be able to park right outside my front door."

This full driveway was the last straw after a long day. Her amateur dramatic society's dress rehearsal had overrun, forcing her to face the supermarket at its busiest time of day, followed by a frustrating rush hour queue at the petrol station.

A third blast of the horn brought nothing except a dirty look from Mr Grainger next door, as he moved his net curtain to see what was going on. Dorothy delved to the bottom of her handbag for her mobile and dialled her own home. It rang and rang before going to the answer machine. She tried again. Ant picked it up on the sixth ring.

"It's pouring with rain," Dorothy shouted against the thunderous noise from Ant's end of the line, "and my drive is littered with strangers' cars. Please get them moved."

"Chill, Grandma, chill. It's no big deal, I'll have a word."

Through the window she saw Ant speak to his student friends. They each peered out into the dark murky weather and then started fumbling in pockets, presumably for keys.

Dorothy had long ago regretted offering Ant somewhere to stay when his university accommodation hadn't materialised. He'd promised it would only be for a week but he was still here almost two months later. She'd only continued to have him for her daughter's sake.

"He's so far from home," Sandra had said. "It's reassuring to know he's got you to turn to – wasn't it lucky that Huddersfield would take him even after he messed up his A' levels?"

Dorothy thought it would've been even luckier if he'd gone to university in his home town instead of her home town. The last couple of months had seen her two-bedroom bungalow invaded by a stream of denim-clad young people of both sexes. On one occasion she'd had to step over bodies scattered across the lounge floor when she went to make her morning tea. Then she'd felt obliged to produce hot drinks and breakfast for everyone.

"Chill, Grandma, chill," Ant said when Dorothy tried to explain how she felt about these strangers. "You're too set in your ways. It'll do you good to loosen up."

After that she'd enforced a 'no overnight visitors' rule. But it wasn't much better when his friends weren't there. Ant spent a surprising amount of time in the bathroom for a male and always left at least 3 wet towels strewn on the floor. The mud from his football kit clogged up the washing machine and he was costing her a fortune in food. She'd given him a final warning a couple of weeks back.

"Start treating my home with respect," she'd demanded, "and pay your way - otherwise you're out!"

"Chill..."

"Do not say those words again!" she'd cut him off mid-sentence.

But he didn't take the warning seriously. The supermarket bill and the number of bags she had to carry from the car to the kitchen continued to grow - which was why she was refusing to walk any further than necessary in this pouring rain.

"How long are these people staying?" Dorothy asked her grandson once the cars had been moved, the music turned down and the shopping put away. "I fancy a long hot bath and Lewis on the television."

"I fancy his side-kick, Hathaway, more," said one of the girls with a giggle, as she walked past them in the hall.

"This is a private conversation," said Dorothy, bristling.

"Chill, Grandma, chill. We're getting ready to go down the pub. But we'll be back later to try some of that chocolate cake I spotted in the tin." He winked at her. "Don't go sharing it with Mr Grainger while we're out!"

Dorothy flushed at the insinuation and then sat tensely in the kitchen whilst the bathroom door opened and closed, music pounded again and her curling tongs were borrowed by the girls.

"Straighteners would've been better," remarked one, "but we'll give these a try."

Eventually the cars left and she took her coffee and paperback into the bathroom. When the taps produced barely warm water, unfamiliar swear words tripped from Dorothy's lips. She could no longer put up with Anthony just to keep Sandra from worrying.

It was time to call her amateur dramatic friends and reclaim her home. The group's costume box would contain what was needed to put her plan into action.

When Ant and his friends returned from the pub, the actors were dressed and ready.

The traffic warden's outfit was dated and slightly too tight for Reg but, in the midnight darkness, Ant and his entourage didn't appear to notice the straining buttons and flared trousers.

"I'm sorry, Sir. This driveway is for permit holders only."

The rain had stopped. Dorothy listened to Reg

through an open window and grinned. From her position behind the curtain she could see Reg brandishing a fake parking ticket at her grandson.

"You can use the parking meters, just down the road, Sir, on the left."

Then, as anticipated, Ant tried to phone Dorothy to complain.

Moira answered the call with a perfect imitation of the speaking clock. Ant tried phoning twice more before giving up and leading the cars to the official parking bays.

Ed opened the door before Ant could put his key in the lock. His nativity innkeeper costume was out of place for the time of year but it fitted the plan.

"Sorry, we have no rooms," Ed said, sombrely.

"Who are you? What are you talking about? Gran!" Ant called into the house. "What about my room?"

"You heard the man - all my rooms are taken," Dorothy said, coming into the hallway and gesturing at her amateur dramatic friends, "and unfortunately I have no stable."

"So what are we supposed to do?"

"Chill, Ant, chill," Dorothy handed her bewildered grandson a fully packed suitcase. "Loosen up and try somewhere new. You don't want to get too set in your ways, do you?"

MY BALLET DANCING RIVAL

"Daddy, Mr Walker can ballet dance!" Emily spins around on her tip toes, steadies herself and then stares up at me with shining eyes. "He said so at Circle Time and he's going to show us in PE."

"That's nice," I say.

Mr Walker is standing in the classroom doorway checking that the correct responsible adult collects each child. He winks at me and I remember the letter that arrived this morning. Emily gives him a big wave as we turn and head towards the school gate.

Pirouetting in a leotard has never appealed to me. Chasing a ball around a muddy field followed by a pint is my thing - but that's not the way to my five-year-old daughter's heart.

It didn't used to matter. I was always her hero. As Emily grew from a wobbly toddler into a chattering, questioning little person she was a daddy's girl. I was the one she ran to with a grazed knee or a tummy-ache. When she swung on my arm and told the old lady next door how she had the best daddy in the world and that he could mend anything from a doll's pram to the stabilisers on her bike, I would smile with fake modesty.

"Daddy's cleverer than you!" she told her Mum at regular intervals, as I shrugged my shoulders and pretended that it was of no consequence to me that our daughter thought I was the bees knees.

"One day she'll learn the truth!" Mandy would tease after I'd been chosen to read the bedtime story yet again. "She'll learn that you're just an ordinary male with smelly habits and are incapable of doing more than one thing at once."

"Jealousy gets you nowhere," was my standard smug reply.

But the point of denouement came sooner than I expected. It began in September when Emily started school and since then, the pedestal on which I stand has diminished rapidly.

Perhaps this morning's news will compensate for my lack of ballet skills or will it just upset her?

Mandy and I have agreed that I will retrain for a new career so that Mandy can eventually work part-time.

"Mr Walker has got two cats!"

We are now walking down the road, away from Mr Walker's lair but still his presence is all around us.

"So why have we only got a goldfish?" Emily demands.

"Cats take a lot of looking after and they'd get lonely when we go on holiday."

"Mr Walker's cats have a cat-flap and go in and out of the house by themselves."

"It sounds like Mr Walker's cats are as clever as he is," I say.

"Don't be silly, Daddy. No one is as clever as Mr Walker!"

We continue in silence for a while.

"Why don't you go to work?" she asks suddenly. "Daddies are supposed to go to work."

Is my five-year-old daughter accusing me of laziness?

"Mummy and I decided our family would work better if she went to work and I stayed at home to look after you."

"But Mr Walker looks after me now, so you can go to work."

I'm about to mention the letter confirming my work placement when she darts off to stroke a cat. I'd been worrying about telling her, thinking she'd be upset about having to attend the after-school club. It seems my worries might be groundless.

"I *am* going to work," I say to her when the cat disappears. "But first I have to learn how to do my new job."

"Mr Walker is very good at making people learn - even the naughty boys who want to play football all the time."

I ignore the insinuation that I might be one of the 'naughty boys'.

"Actually," I say, "Mr Walker knows all about my new job."

"You see!" She is triumphant. "Mr Walker knows everything!"

"I'm going to be a teacher. Next term I'm going to help Mr Walker in the classroom before I go to college for my training."

Emily's face is a picture of amazement and then she suddenly looks aghast.

"But you don't know how to ballet dance! You have to know for PE." She grabs my hand. "Quick, let's get home and I'll show you."

ALSO BY SALLY JENKINS

The Promise

A man has been stabbed. A woman is bloodstained. The nightmares from her teenage years have begun again for Olivia Field – just as she is preparing to marry.

Ex-convict, Tina is terminally ill. Before she dies, the care of her younger, psychologically unwell brother, Wayne must be ensured. So Tina calls in a promise made to her thirty years ago in a prison cell. A promise that was written down and placed with crucial evidence illustrating a miscarriage of justice in a murder case.

The Promise is a fast-paced psychological thriller told from several viewpoints. It explores the lengths to which people are prepared go in order to protect those they love and the impossibility of ever fully escaping our past actions.

Reviewers' praise for The Promise:
"I didn't see the ending coming." – Hellymart.
"I quickly found myself in the "I'll just read one more chapter" loop." – Whiskas Mum.
"A brilliant, pacey thriller with an interesting plot line." – Bookliterati.

Bedsit Three

A girl has been buried in a shallow grave. Rain washes away the earth covering her. *Bedsit Three* is a thrilling why-dunnit which twists and turns its way to a shattering finale! No one knows what goes on behind closed doors or in the darkness of our minds. Sometimes the threat is too close to home ...

Bedsit Three is a tale of murder, mystery and love. It won the inaugural Wordplay Publishing/Ian Govan Award and was shortlisted for both the Silverwood-Kobo-Berforts Open Day Competition and the Writing Magazine/McCrit Competition.

Michael Barton, Founder and Managing Director of WordPlay Publishing said of Bedsit Three, "It's a book that elicits emotional reaction, drawing the reader into the story and placing him or her in the middle of the action page after page. Be prepared for a sleepless night, because you won't want to put it down until you get to the end."

Reviewers' praise for Bedsit Three:

"A psychological why dunnit reminiscent of Barbara Vine/ Ruth Rendell. Highly recommended!" Elizabeth Barnsley

"A dark, fairly gritty drama with a side plot of insanity and murder - I enjoyed it!" – Terry Tyler

Printed in Great Britain
by Amazon

73766368R00132